THUGLIT

Issue One

Edited by Todd Robinson

THUGLIT

These are works of fiction. Names, characters, corporations, institutions, organizations, events, or locales in the works are either the product of the author's imagination or, if real, used fictitiously. The resemblance of any character to actual persons (living or dead) is entirely coincidental.

THUGLIT: Issue One

Stories by the authors: ©Todd Robinson, ©Johnny Shaw, ©Jordan Harper, ©Court Merrigan, ©Mike Wilkerson, ©Hilary Davidson, ©Jason Duke, ©Matthew C Funk, ©Terrence McCauley

Published by THUGLIT Publishing

ISBN-13:
978-1480182998

ISBN-10:
1480182990

Issue 1

THUGLIT

Issue 1

Table of Contents

Welcome (back?) to Thuglit

I'm gonna break down this introduction into two parts to avoid confusion—first part is for the Newbies. A welcome, a how-do-ya-do to the world of the wicked that is Thuglit. The other half is for...you know who you are. You know why you're here. Let's get started, shall we?

NEWBIES

How ya doin? New around these parts? Lemme tell ya, you're in the right place...or the worst place imaginable, depending on your sensibilities. But I'm going to plow right ahead and assume that you're reading a mag like Thuglit because you've heard of us and like your literature like we do—nasty.

You haven't heard of us? Well, in our previous incarnation, we ran for five years, then went on hiatus for the last two years. We published some early work from some of the best crime fiction scribblers on the planet. We won so many dang awards that we lost count.

Seriously.

We don't fuck around.

What you're about to delve into is some short fiction that will make your head spin, your heart race, and your grandma weep.

And if you're like us, you're gonna love every goddamn word.

If that's the case? Welcome. You're beginning a journey into the unwashed alley of crime fiction where the men are men, the women are women, the men are sometimes women, the women play with the big boys, and everybody's intentions lean to the unsavory.

If you're not? Go back down into your Mom's basement and blog away about how you've just wasted your Taco Bell wages.

Haters gonna hate.

THUGKETEERS

How's it been, babies?

You miss us?

Aw, now…don't be like that. We missed you too.

C'mere.

Closer.

You know you wanted this. That's why you're here. That's why you came back. I know you was mad, but we had to go away for a while. We needed some space.

But now we're back and it's gonna be better than ever. You smell nice…

We missed you too. *Mmmm*, reader, you feel so *good*. I wanna get up in your occipital-temporal cortex where your voluptuous brain processes written language and thrust these words all deep inside you. Can you feel it? Can you feel how much I want to do it?

That sound good babies?

That *feeeel* good?

And now that I've creeped everybody the hell out: *Enjoy, bitches!*

Todd Robinson (Big Daddy Thug)
08/30/2012

Lucy in the Pit
by Jordan Harper

If she pisses, she lives.

Lucy's gums are bone-white, whiter that the teeth set into them. It is a sign of shock. Her body is shutting down, one system at a time. Kidneys close shop first. If she pisses, it means her body is starting up again. If she doesn't, her blood will fill with poisons and she will die.

If Lucy was my dog I would not have matched her against Tuna. Four pounds is a serious advantage for a sixty-pound dog. It should have been a forfeit. But Jesse needed the money. I told myself that I let him get his way because he is Lucy's owner and I am just her handler.

Icy wind off Lake Erie rocks the truck, making me swerve. I pull my hand back from Lucy's mouth and put it back on the wheel. I must drive steady. I must not speed. I cannot risk the police pulling us over. Lucy would die on the side of the road while I sat helpless in handcuffs.

Lucy's fur is the color of a bad day. Deep grey turned to black where the blood soaks her. Her blood is everywhere. There is gauze over a bad bleeder on the thick muscles of her neck where Tuna savaged her. I wanted to end the fight then, pick Lucy up and declare Tuna the victor. But Jesse said no. Again I let him win. And Lucy scratched the floor trying to get back in the fight.

Tough little bitch. Proud little warrior.

She cannot fight again. Her front leg will never be the same. After tonight she can retire, she can breed, she can heal. But she isn't done yet. We both have a fight waiting for us in the hotel room.

*****

I am a dogman. I breed fighting dogs. I train fighting dogs to fight better. I take fighting dogs to their fights and I handle them in the pit. This is what I do. It may not be your way but it is an old way. My father was a dogman. He learned the trade from my grandfather, and he taught it to me. I have seen dogs fight and bleed and die. I have cheered them on as they fought. It can be cruel.

There are dog-fighters who beat their dogs, who whip them and starve them thinking to make the dogs savage. There's those who kill their curs, who drown them or shock them and then burn their bodies in the backyard. Some men fight their dogs to the death every time, no quarter asked for or given. Some men fight their dogs in garbage-strewn alleys with rats watching on greedily, the rats knowing they'll get to feed on the corpse of the loser.

There is another way. In a real dog match, the kind that still draws its rules from old issues of *The Police Gazette*, there's a ring about fourteen feet square. Each side has a line in the dirt, a scratch line. You set the dogs behind their scratch lines and hold on to their collars good and tight. You let them go. Each time there's a break in the action you pull those dogs apart and put them back behind their scratch lines. If one of the dogs doesn't scratch the earth, running in place to get back into it, the fight is over. No dog fights that doesn't want it. It has to more than want it—it has to claw for it, it has to want it like the fight was a chunk of steak or a piece of pussy.

When a dog doesn't scratch, the fight is over. A dog that gives up, you call that a "cur." Dogs that don't have any cur in them, we call them "game dogs." Dogs that scratch even when they're close to death, who'd rather die than give up, you call those dogs "dead game."

But you don't let them die, not if you're a real dogman. A dead game dog is the goal, the pinnacle of a pit dog. That needs to breed. To make more dead game dogs. To breed more warrior stock. You've got to be the quit for a dog who doesn't have quit in them. A man who lets a dead game dog fight to the death is both cruel and foolish.

My employer is a cruel and foolish man.

You may think that I am cruel and foolish too. Maybe you want to think I'm the villain of this story. And maybe I am. But now I'm going to tell you about Lucy. And hers is a story worth telling.

*****

The hotel where I have built my emergency room sits in one of those Detroit neighborhoods where it looks like a slow-motion bomb has been exploding for the last thirty years. Even the people are torn apart. I see crutches, wheelchairs, missing limbs. Nothing and no one are complete.

I pull off of Van Dyke into the lot of the Coral Court. Hookers, tricks and pimps scatter like chickens. The tires crunch on asphalt chunks and broken glass. I park as close to the room as I can.

I leave Lucy in the cab of the truck and open the door to the room I have rented. It is just how I left it. One of the double beds has been stripped down, a fresh sheet of my own laid across it. I crank the thermostat up to max. Lucy will need the heat.

I wrap Lucy in a towel and carry her across the lot. She is so small and so cold. As we cross the lot, a fat man drinking from a brown paper bag shoots me a look.

"Goddamn, what'd you do to that dog?"

"Put your eyes back in your head, motherfucker," I tell him. He looks away. So cur he can't even see I'm bluffing.

I take Lucy inside. I place her on the sheet. The white sheet blushes as it soaks up her blood. I open up the tackle box that serves as my mobile medical kit. I change the gauze on her neck. I tape it on tight. I take out a long loop of bootlace. I tourniquet the front leg, the one with the most bleeders. I take out a brown plastic bottle of hydrogen peroxide. I yank out the marlinspike on my knife and stab through the lid. I wash out the wounds. Dozens of punctures, tears, jaw-shaped rings all over the front of her.

They say that Vlad the Impaler walked through the field hospitals after battle, inspecting the wounded. Those with wounds to the front of them got promoted. Those with wounds in their backs, like they'd been fleeing—Vlad had those men killed. Vlad would have made Lucy a general. Her back and haunches are unmarred. She'd fought every second she'd been in the bout.

Tough little bitch. Proud little warrior.

*****

The match had been in an abandoned warehouse—no shortage of those here. The ring had been built in the morning out of a two-foot tall square of wood filled up halfway with dirt. Around the ring stood gangbangers, bikers, cholos and mobbed-up types. Dog matches in Detroit are like those ads by that one clothes company that always have the black guy and the white guy holding hands, except at the dog match the other hand is filled with blood money or a gun.

Tuna was owned by Frankie Arno, who lived in St. Clair Shores along with all the other Detroit dagos who didn't get the memo that the Mafia doesn't run things anymore. His dogman was Deets from the Cass Corridor.

Deets doesn't hold to the old ways. Deets uses a homemade electric chair to fry his curs, and hangs live cats from chains for his dogs to chew on and improve their grips. When the referee told us that Tuna came in heavy, I told Jesse to kill the match.

"Four pounds is too much," I told him.

"Fuck that," Jesse said. "You told me this bitch is game."

He was a short man with a short man's temper. He was the only man I've ever known to lose money in the drug trade. He bought Lucy and some other prime stock when he was flush. He also hired the best dogman in Michigan, if you don't mind me calling myself that. Now that he was down, he was looking to recoup his investment. I do not know who he owes money to, only that they are frightening to this frightening man. This type of fear doesn't make a man listen to reason. I tried anyway.

"She is," I said. "She has potential to be a grand champion. That's worth more money than one fight."

"I'm not bitching out here. I'm not a punk."

Across the ring, Deets studied us behind hooded eyes. Deets knew Jesse needed the purse money. Deets knew that I wouldn't be able to talk Jesse out of the match if Deets brought his dog in heavy. Four pounds wasn't a mistake. It was strategy. I had to hand it to him. He'd played it beautifully. I gave him a nod to let him know. He just kept staring back.

Before a match, each side's handlers wash the other one's dog. Keeps a man like Deets from soaking his dog's fur with poison. Back in the old days, the rule was you could ask to taste a man's dog if you were suspicious. I didn't like handling Tuna, much less licking her. I know the signs of a dog who has been treated mean. When I washed her she trembled, and a deep-chest growl burbled in her chest. It sounded like a boat idling at the dock. Pit dogs shouldn't growl at a man. We breed them to love us. I didn't want to know what Deets had done to her to ruin that. She kept growling but she didn't bite me. Maybe it would have been better if she had. If she'd bit we'd have put her down right there. That's one way our world and the straight world agrees: Dogs that attack men have to go.

But instead I took Lucy to one end of the ring and Deets took Tuna to the other end. Lucy, who had licked my face with a dog's smile just a minute before, strained to get away from me to head into the fight. The fight is a pit dog's highest purpose. We have bred them to not feel fear or pain. We have bred them to have wide jaws and a low center of gravity. A pit dog wants the fight the way a ratter wants the rat, the way a bloodhound wants the scent. A dead game dog wants it more than they want life.

On the signal from the referee I released my hold on Lucy. The two dogs collided with a slap and the sound of snapping teeth. Otherwise the warehouse was quiet. The spectators at a dog match are like the men at a strip club. Sometimes they cheer and clap, but mostly they stare on in silence, lost in their own private world.

In the fight there's nothing for a handler to do but watch. You can't teach a pit dog to fight any more than you can teach a horse to run. You exercise the dog, but the dog teaches itself. There are many ways of dog fighting, styles as different as the kung-fu styles in those old movies. Some dogs are leg biters. Some go for the head. Some dogs use muscle and buzzsaw speed, while others fight smart. Some just latch onto the bottom jaw and hang on until the other dog burns itself out and gives up. Some dogs are killers whose opponents don't get the chance to give up. They tear throats and end lives.

Tuna was a killer. She went for the throat. She had a good, strong mouth that tore Lucy up. She had four pounds on her, enough to bully her into position.

Lucy was the smartest dog I ever saw in the pit. She rode Tuna around, denied her the killing grip. Lucy turned the overweight bitch into a leg-biter. But Lucy couldn't get her own holds to stick. Tuna muscled out of them each time. Thirty minutes into the fight Tuna worked herself out of Lucy's grasp and sank her jaws into Lucy's neck. She shook Lucy, trying for a tighter grip, and Lucy slid under her, got her claws into Tuna's belly and twisted herself free. As the dogs repositioned themselves, bloody, winded, I told Jesse to pick Lucy up. The fight was over, I told him.

"Are you fucking kidding me?" Jesse asked. "No way."

I could have picked her up then. I should have. But I didn't.

It took her another half-hour and maybe her life, but Lucy finally broke the bigger dog. When Tuna went cur and we pulled Lucy off her, Lucy was still clawing to get at the beaten dog.

Tough little bitch. Proud little warrior.

It wasn't until later, while Jesse counted his money, that the adrenaline went away and Lucy collapsed.

*****

If she pisses, she lives. So I need to get fluids into her system. I take out a plastic bag of saline. I stick it under my armpit to warm it up for a minute. I hook the IV up onto the metal stand. I take Lucy's leg in my hand and roll my thumb around it until the vein is visible against the bone of the leg. I wipe Lucy down with an alcohol swab. I get the IV needle out. I go to put the needle in. I stop.

My hand is shaking. Dumb animal panic. I stare at it for long seconds. I take a few deep breaths. The shaking subsides. I slide the needle in. I secure it with horse tape. I take the IV bag out of my armpit and hook it to the IV.

Next I give Lucy a shot of an anti-inflammatory drug, pre-measured out for 20 milligrams per kilogram of bodyweight. Next, penicillin, 1cc per twenty pounds of bodyweight. While the fluids go in her, I get back to treating her wounds. I trim the hanging skin to keep the flesh from going proud. I check her mouth to see if she has bitten through her lips. Her gums are the whitish-pink of fresh veal. Better. Not good enough.

I close the wounds. Some bites just get a little powder. I get out the staple gun for the worst of them. They bind the wounds together with a great loud *CLICK*. Lucy does not wince or whine while the staples snap down on her flesh.

Tough little bitch. Proud little warrior.

*****

I will not let her die. But there's nothing I can do now. I have to give the fluids a chance to work. She sleeps. I can't. I watch bad teevee, something with fat people sweating on treadmills. I switch channels. People screaming at each other, throwing glasses, throwing punches. I switch again. The news, nothing but lying politicians and pretty dead white girls.

A knock at the door. I check out the peephole. It's Jesse. I open the door. A miasma of whiskey-stink comes in with him. He looks at Lucy. He whistles a low note.

"She still living?"

"For now."

"Do what you can, man," he says. "She's hardcore. Me likey."

"She'll be a hell of dam," I say. I'm talking too fast. I never was a salesman. "Let's breed her with that brindle stud that Lopez has…"

"Hell, no, not yet. Bitch has fights in her yet."

"Jesse, she'll never come back all the way from this," I say. "She's already going to be a legend. Four pounds over and the dead game bitch won. Breed her."

"She's going back in the pit," he says. I chew a chunk out of the side of my mouth.

"That rapper dude who was there, the one who owns Cherry? He wants to match her," Jesse says. "Shit, man, Cherry's a grand champion. She's legit."

"Lucy's leg won't ever heal right. She can't win another fight."

"Fuck it, then we lay money on her to lose. It's still getting paid."

I don't say anything. My hands are shaking again. I don't want Jesse to see.

"Palmer?" He looks at me.

"She can't go back in the pit," I tell him. I try to sound calm and steady.

"What's this *can't* shit?" Jesse turns his body sideways. It's an unconscious reaction of a fighting man to a threat. You turn sideways to make your body a smaller target to your enemy. I think about the stories I've heard. The things Jesse's done to men who cross him. Stories with knives in them. Pliers. Heated pieces of metal.

There is a scratch line in front of me.

I do not scratch. I do not fight.

"I'm your dogman," I tell him. "You're the owner. You make the call. If she lives, Jesse. Big If."

His posture goes back to normal. He smiles.

"That's the spirit. If she dies, she dies. But if not, patch her up and we match her against Cherry. The gate will be enormous. Anyway, I didn't get into this to be a breeder, like some bored Grosse Pointe housewife with her goddamn Pekinese. I'm in it for the blood. Win or lose it's a payday, isn't it?"

I say "Yeah."

Cur. Goddamn cur.

Jesse leaves. I look towards Lucy. Lucy's ribs rise and fall so gently. If she lives, she will not recover fast enough. She will lose her next match. Lucy is dead game. She will not quit until she is dead. And Jesse won't pull her out.

If she pisses, she lives. But then what? She fights. She dies. Dies bad.

I'm saving her life to kill her in a month.

Tough little bitch. Proud little warrior.

I'm sorry I am not as strong as you.

Issue 1

At the bottom of the tackle box is the final treatment. Vets call it T-61. It's a fatal mixture of narcotics and paralytics, legally available only to licensed veterinarians. If I inject the T-61 into the IV bag, Lucy never has to wake up again. I take the plastic stopper off of the T-61.

The IV continues its *drip-drip-drip*. Lucy stirs. Her legs run in dog dreaming, swaddling up the blanket around her. She snarls. She bites the air. Still fighting in her sleep.

Still fighting.

Ok then. We'll do it her way.

*****

I carry Lucy out into the parking lot and lay her down. She sniffs the ground weakly. Her paws shake with the effort. She looks up at me with pleading eyes. She knows what I want of her. But she is so very tired. She falls into the gravel. Some of her wounds open up again. Blood drips, but no piss.

I'm talking to her. I don't know when I started. I don't know exactly what I tell her, but I know that it is true. The world fades out around us until we are the only two things left in it. I make her a promise. I know that I mean it.

I will not let her die.

Lucy squats. My heart sits too large in my chest. It kicks and kicks. Lucy yelps. She squirts hot amber piss onto the parking lot. A flood of it.

Tough little bitch. Proud little warrior.

When she is done Lucy limps over to my side and leans against me, confused by the noises I can't help making. I stand in the hotel parking lot and cry over a puddle of dog piss.

I made her a promise. I will keep it. Lucy will not fight again. She's fought enough. Me? I'm just getting started. If

Jesse has a problem with that, he better be ready to scratch.

We'll see who is cur.

Bastards of Apathy

by Jason Duke

Nothing would keep the egg from frying on the sidewalk—Angel Rodriguez was that cocksure about it. He looked to the sky where the smog had turned the desert sky from blue to hazy green. The noon sun hung brutal like a furnace over Angel's head, blasting down on him through the smog.

His homeboy Lauro Cavazos stood next to the gleaming metal statue of the Phoenix (called *Garfield Rising*), the statue donated by the young hipster artists a block up Roosevelt Street at Alwun House as a symbol of the efforts to gentrify Garfield district. Their motto: using the power of art to transform community. The metal bird rose from a nest of metal flames, screeching down on Angel like it wanted badly to peck out his eyes.

Just in case, Angel kissed the egg for luck. He said a little silent prayer to let him win the bet with Lauro because money was always at the top of the list of things to pray for. Then he shotgunned the egg so hard at the rusted metal pedestal the Phoenix was perched on, he felt the air snap, saw the little sonic boom part the oven heat rising on the air.

The egg sizzled. Lauro stooped to the alligatored sidewalk; put his face near the egg.

But nothing happened.

"It isn't frying."

"Just wait."

The edges fried.

Angel cradled the carton in his free arm, jumping up and down.

"See, I told you! Pay up motherfucker!"

Lauro slapped twenty dollars in Angel's palm.

Jesus, it was fucking hot! Lauro thought, squinting at the sun. The fact he was short, stocky, and chubby didn't help him, not in the slightest.

But hot enough to fry an egg on the sidewalk?

Lauro would never have guessed it. Now his ignorance cost him twenty dollars.

"What the fuck? That's some bullshit, man," Lauro was laughing.

Angel shrugged, "Seeing is believing."

*****

It was hotter mid-July heat than Lauro had experienced last year, after moving to the desert with his mother. As he squinted at the sun, he considered Angel probably knew exactly how hot it needed to get for the egg to fry. Angel had the advantage of being born and raised in Phoenix, living there longer.

They hopped the fence to Garfield Elementary; cut across the sallow playfield. They put as much distance as they could between them and their crime, where the metal Phoenix sat on the other side of the black vertical bar fence.

Like a game of follow the leader, Angel led Lauro through the neighborhood. They kept an eye out for cops; larger groups of teens. They took a shortcut through a ramshackle stucco duplex with a giant banner hung from the side, advertising: *Low rent, low move-in fees.*

On Fillmore, the next street over, they passed a beautifully renovated pyramidal cottage that had been boarded up and a For Sale sign stuck in the yard. The cottage was wedged into a row of broken-down ranch style homes and empty dirt lots. Another home was boarded up, missing a door, the insides gutted, the copper pipes and wires picked clean. Slivers of shade bordered the sides of the buildings, or under the moribund fronds of wayward palm trees leaning hunched along the broken street like the bowed backs of old, tired men.

Angel was tossing an egg in the air, catching it. Across the street, a skinny girl with ratty matted hair squatted in the feeble shade of the boarded up home with the missing door.

When he noticed her, his first impression was: crack whore squatting to piss. She had a greasy dirt-streaked face, dirty clothes, like she belonged in a third world country—not America.

What was she doing there? He wondered if she was really taking a piss.

Maybe he would get a free show.

"You know her?"

"Nope, never seen her before," Lauro said.

Angel lobbed the egg near her.

She ran to a white mini-van covered in rust spots, missing a rear bumper.

A man, her father by the looks of it, jumped out of the back of van as she got inside with the rest of her family.

They were huddled around ice chests, piles of clothes. Angel saw the black trash bags filled with everything they owned.

The children had their faces buried in their mother's arms.

He yelled, "Go park at a Walmart!"

The dad got in the van, drove away.

Lauro laughed, uneasily, "That's cold, man."

*****

Inside Verde Park, near the Verde Community Center, the preteens were playing, catcalling to Miss Padilla again in their squeaky little voices. "Hey mamacita! I want to do the wild thing to you!"

Another said, "How much for a blowjob, bitch?"

In unsure voices that could crack glass, they catcalled, giggled. They tossed their football back and forth.

Miss Padilla, she couldn't remember faces anymore. Her life before she got clean last year made it so. But the kids would not let her forget. She still liked to straddle her neck in gold jewelry. She still liked to wear the same hot pink, skin-tight, halter-top dress.

Angel said, "Check out Miss Padilla. Baby got back."

At a fast clip, she bustled up Van Buren Street. Her chest puffed out, tits bouncing all over the place.

He did a little bump and grind dance, dry fucking the air. "I wouldn't mind riding that train."

"You'd fuck her? She's like forty, and she used to be a prostitute."

"I'm just playin'."

Lauro smiled, "What're you getting your mom for her birthday? Something nice?"

"I was thinking of some gold jewelry."

Miss Padilla wore giant gold earrings that glinted in the sun.

Lauro saw the gold around her neck.

"I fucking dare you! You won't do it!"

She bustled toward them like daring them to stop her, daring them to do something about it. But without looking them in the eye, she strutted past. Angel grabbed the jewelry from her neck. She started screaming, "Fuckin' no good rotten kids!" Then she was shouting, *"Fuckin' no good rotten kids!"*

Issue 1

Before they knew it was happening, she had opened her Chanel purse, pulled a gun. She boomed the way thunderclaps rumble through clouds, across the sky, "I'm gonna teach you not to fuck with decent folk!"

Without thinking, Angel ran. It didn't register in Lauro's mind right away that Angel had run. Lauro bolted a second later, as fast as his fat little legs would carry him. He was too slow, and it was all the excuse she needed to shoot him twice in his back with the .38 snub-nosed revolver. Like a spooked stampeding cow, Lauro belly-flopped into the ground. The momentum of his dead weight carried him skidding across the scarred pavement on his chin.

She boomed, squeezing off the last four shots in the revolver, *"Fuckin' no good rotten kids!"*

She waved the gun, blasts cutting the palpable heat rising on the air. Inside Verde Park the kids screamed, fell, one by one as the errant bullets struck them.

Fuckin' no good rotten kids!

Angel didn't look back. He just kept running all the way to Washington Street where the metro light rail thrummed in place, its doors open. Had the train been waiting for him? He didn't have time to consider it. Not that he cared, and jumped inside.

*****

The Ikea was both colossal and confusing. There was so much shit to buy, Brandy Ashton didn't know where to begin. Some of the displays looked very modern to her, and hinted of a future that would leave her behind in the dust unless she bought something. Also, she noticed the only way to get through the store was by taking the longest route possible.

Brandy realized what the mad architects behind the maze were cleverly doing; resented them for it. Though it

19

was her first visit to the store, she wondered why she had even bothered.

Finally, she settled on a Bolman 3-piece bathroom set, a Svalen bath towel (the one with the angry fish with the sharp teeth), and an Idealisk corkscrew. She had been saving an exquisite bottle of Beringer White Zinfandel all month, and bought some brie that morning to pair with the wine. Thinking on the wine paired with the cheese, she tingled.

But then she thought of the long bus ride home. The #65 bus she had taken from the metro light rail—how she would have to wait another ungodly amount of time on the bus going back. She thought again of the wine, the cheese, and everything was okay.

"Excuse me?" Brandy said to the girl at the work station. Her name was Erica according to her nametag.

Sullenly, Erica looked at Brandy.

"Can you help me?" Brandy finally said, wondering if she broke a two-by-four over Erica's head, would it wake her up? "I have a question about that entertainment center over there."

Erica glanced back at the copy of *Cosmopolitan* (underneath: *Rolling Stone*). She closed the magazine, as if helping Brandy was a waste of her time. The disdain was written on her pretty, young face: how dare she be bothered.

Brandy said, "How much is it? There's no ticket on it."

"Two hundred and twenty-five dollars."

"Is it available?"

"Yes, but we don't have the bottom doors in," motioning to the bottom cabinets. "They won't be in until Saturday. You'll have to come back if you want them."

"Is there any way to have the doors delivered?" Brandy asked.

"No."

Surprised, Brandy said, "There's no way to have them delivered? What about the floor model, is it for sale?"

"No," said Erica, annoyed, trying to hide it.

"Is there a manager available?"

Erica gave a look that said: I can't believe you're wasting my time with this. No longer trying to hide it, she said annoyed, "Why do you want to talk to a manager?"

"Why do I have to explain myself to you?"

Now Erica had the look of a person holding their breath: that frozen, bated breath expression when something totally unexpected is said and they are trying to figure out what to say next, how to respond.

More than anything, Brandy hated dealing with these kids. Spoiled, bratty kids who acted like they were owed the world. Erica looked fresh out of high school—young, pretty; but Brandy knew, attitude trumped looks, any day. She had at least fifteen years on Erica, and still, she looked just as good. The only difference were the little crow's feet growing at the edges of Brandy's eyes that perhaps betrayed her age.

She waited for Erica to say something. Finally, she said, "Because you're not being very helpful. Maybe there's something the manager can—"

Erica talked over her, "We can deliver the doors. Where do you live?"

"The west valley."

"We can deliver them, but it's going to cost you eighty-nine dollars."

"So they can be delivered? Why didn't you tell me that in the first place? I still want to see the manager."

So, little Erica made the call. Talking a few minutes on the phone, she said, "The manager will be here in ten minutes, if you still want to wait."

Go fuck yourself.

That was the look on Brandy's face.

Jesus, she hated dealing with these kids. She wished she had that two-by-four. Right now, she wanted nothing more than to bash in Erica's pretty little face.

The gold chain called to Brandy, from her neck. The same simple gold chain her mother had passed to her when she was a little girl.

Momma Ashton—on her deathbed, dying of cancer—had passed the heirloom to her only daughter the way her mother, and her grandmother, and her great-grandmother had done generations past, all the way down the family line, to the very first Ashtons that had settled in the northeast (what possessed them to move and settle in Arizona, she would never understand).

When the first Ashtons arrived penniless in America, they kept the gold chain no matter the indigence or hardship, as a symbol of providence, and reminder that fortunes were made through diligence and hard work.

Brandy stormed off, so furious she wanted to cry.

No one looking, she stroked the gold chain and felt better. Stroking the thin gold chain always had a calming, soothing effect. There was nothing she would not do to protect that chain, to keep it in the family, in the hopes of one day passing the heirloom to her own daughter.

On her way through the winding maze, Brandy spied a fat woman with long hair down to her hips, long denim dress down past her knees. The woman was asking one of the employees for help.

He told her he would be along to help her in a minute.

Then he turned his back on her to answer his cell phone.

His name was Mark, according to his nametag—another punk kid: no surprise there. Whether his thin beard growing in patches was the result of a recent choice to grow one, or because he was still too young, she wasn't sure.

No, she decided, it was because he was still too young.

Frustrated, the poor lady walked away. Brandy followed her out of the maze, into the warehouse. Waiting at one of the bins was the woman's fat mother.

Issue 1

Why were there so many fat people in America, Brandy wondered?

Together, they tried unsuccessfully removing one of the giant boxes from the bin.

As they did, a man passed by with a cart, said, "Need some help? Here, let me help you with that."

He was late thirties, Brandy guessed. Not much older than her, and handsome. The ladies thanked him—bless his heart, they said. They cautioned him against straining his back.

"No problem," he smiled.

Bless his heart, they said.

The kid's phone call was more important than doing his job.

Thank you for doing Ikea's job, because that is the level of professionalism you can expect from Ikea.

So go fuck yourself Ikea! Fuck you in the ass!

Brandy stopped the rant playing in her mind.

Stroking her gold chain, she felt better.

*****

Twenty minutes late, the #65 bus still had not arrived. Brandy stroked her gold chain. She hated waiting on the bus almost as much as she hated dealing with punk kids. She wondered what more could go wrong today? When would the day end?

She looked to all the Marks, the Ericas, crowded at the bus stop. Badly, she wanted to whack them with her shopping bag.

They gossiped about Justin Bieber's love child; the latest Twilight film. How Lady Gaga's keen fashion sense, latest fashion statements, were all the rave:

I'm team Jacob!

I'm team Edward!

How a meat dress was so nouveau— risqué.

Jesus Christ! When was the fucking bus coming?

Then—salvation! The bus appeared around the corner. It rumbled up the street and, with whining airbrakes and long hiss of air, slowed at the bus stop.

Brandy sighed, grateful the noise had severed the grape vine, put a stop to the buzzing rumor mill. She was amazed how animated, fast-talking, these kids could be in the unbearable heat.

Obnoxiously, one of the Erica's said, "Hello? Do you mind?"

The bus doors had opened, Brandy realized. She was blocking the way.

All the Marks, the Ericas, shoved past. Brandy quietly boarded onto the bus, with the rest of the adults.

With disgusted but resigned looks, they quietly boarded. Obediently they fed their money to the money feeder while the kids continued their inane gossiping.

They filed onto the bus, one after the other until all were on board.

As they did, two young men horseplaying in the aisle nearly knocked over an old lady trying to make her way to the back. None of the unruly youngsters offered up their seats so the older folk could sit, rest. Nothing was said.

That would be them some day, Brandy relished: forced to ride the bus to their retail jobs—or their jobs waiting tables—because their cars had been repossessed. Or rather because they could not afford a car to begin with.

Jesus, she realized she just described her own pathetic life. How long had she been working at Macy's, anyway?

It occurred to her the only jobs around anymore were those working behind a counter, or behind a bar, or waiting on tables in a restaurant; the Walmart-type jobs. Or, if you were lucky, cleaning bedpans in a hospital.

"Hey, watch it! You almost knocked her down," one of the kids spoke up.

"Fuck you!"

"Mind your own business, fucker!"

Issue 1

When the metro light rail doors opened, Angel Rodriguez crammed into the train. Into the thick crowd of passengers.

Squeezing next to Brandy, she sighed loud.

It had taken her forever riding the #65 bus to reach the light rail, putting up with all those rude, obnoxious punk kids the entire time.

Now she would have to spend god knew how long on the light rail next to another punk kid.

He said nothing back.

Maybe he hadn't heard her sigh, she guessed.

Thank god, she thought to herself when she caught a glimpse of him. Spying on him from the corner of her eye, she tried not to look obvious doing it.

Her first impression was: evil gang-banger. The fact alone that he wore baggy clothes spelled trouble and meant he was likely no good. But then again, she realized, all the boys wore baggy clothes nowadays. The girls: unbelievably tight clothes, the little whores.

Etched in the window glass, she eyed a piece of graffiti. All the money spent on the light rail, to help people get around easier, improve their lives and the environment, some asshole writes graffiti on the train.

Some asshole like him, Brandy figured.

She wished Honda hadn't recalled their airbags. Then she wouldn't be in this mess, standing next to this devil. How much longer would it take Honda to fix her car, she wondered? Was that fire in his eyes? Did she actually see flames? And tiny horns?

How much longer must she put up with public transportation?

If it wasn't her car getting recalled, it was always something.

The train jolted; everyone swayed with the movement, like water vacillated in a bowl.

Angel jostled against Brandy, and she could swear she felt him grope her tits as he did.

Then, quickly he moved away. But the crowd was so thick, he only managed a few feet.

Again, Brandy thought on the exquisite bottle of Beringer White Zinfandel. The one she had saved all month.

Suddenly, everything was okay.

She went to stroke her gold chain, looked down at her violated tits, and saw the chain was gone.

Grinning, he looked her over. She could feel his fiery eyes on her.

Among the nest of gold chains about his neck, she saw her chain: the little cocky, arrogant prick!

He had stolen her chain!

Now he was grinning, daring her to do something about it.

Over the intercom, the next stop was announced. The doors opened.

Brandy waited.

The doors closed; Brandy grabbed all the chains from Angel's neck. She leapt from the train!

The daring leap thrilled her. Snatching the chains from Angel's neck, taking back what was rightfully hers.

It was exhilarating.

She felt more alive than she'd ever been.

Then Angel was prying the doors open.

She felt cast into some surreal horror flick, her world turned upside down. Wedging one arm through the gap, he pried the doors open. Then his other arm was through.

The train pulled away, picking up speed. No, he was not going to make it.

Please, she prayed—

no, no, no, no.

Thank god, she was saved.

Issue 1

He pried open the doors and, jumping from the train, he looked to Brandy with eyes like murderous slits against the glaring sun.

Screaming, she ran.

Angel chased on her heels, shouting, "You're fucking dead bitch when I catch you!"

Her shopping bag flopped wildly at her side.

She ran—so fast—the people, and storefronts, and the buildings she ran past, blurred into ghostly echoes.

To her, all that mattered was running, staying alive.

She ran—faster, harder.

Then rounded a corner and—

—ran straight into an alley.

*****

The world caught up to her, upside down.

Everything slammed into focus at the mouth of the alley.

Angel lifted her by her waist, as if she were filled with air; threw her face-first to the pavement. Her cheek broke like porcelain against the alley.

Inside her face, she felt the shattered bone slide around. She tasted blood, opened her mouth. The blood squirted out.

"Fucking bitch!"

Turning Brandy over, her gold chain fell from her cleavage. She started crying.

"Oh my god! I'm so sorry! I thought you stole it!"

She gargled on the blood, spilled it from her mouth, "Please! I didn't know! Oh my god! I'm so sorry!"

He hammer-fisted her face.

Why would no one help her, she wondered? Where were all the good Samaritans, the cops to her rescue? Her eyes swelled shut.

The last thing she saw before her eyes closed was the young hipster artist drinking from his cup of Starbucks.

Finally, her knight in shining armor had arrived.

"Not my problem," the kid hurried past.

Across the street, the Marks, the Ericas, were taping her murder on their cell phones.

Her forehead, swollen and gigantic, looked ready to burst.

Her eyes: puffy, blood-filled black sacks.

"Fucking bitch!"

Angel stomped on her stomach. He jumped up, down on her stomach.

He jumped up and down on her chest, missed, and almost fell over.

Kicking her in the head, her neck snapped.

Then he jumped up, stomped on her face, and her nose crunched into her face. The kids across the street gasped, but kept taping.

*****

Angel held the gold chains up to the sun.

The gold glinted in the sunlight, and Brandy's chain caught his eye.

From his doorway, Momma Rodriguez waved to him: the run-down, Spanish colonial revival.

It was midway along the broken street, the cracked sidewalks. Worn concrete the city of Phoenix had neglected fixing, or had forgotten alltogether to fix.

The little hovel, where they eked out their living.

Same as the rest of the dirt-poor residents of Garfield district, the ones lucky still to have homes.

He thought on the little ratty crack girl; her homeless family...

...fuck them!

bitch he'd stomped in...

...fuck them!

Issue 1

On beating that uppity bitch to death, he felt some remorse. The cell phone tapings would likely catch up with him, he realized.

He regretted that most.

Not that any of those kids cared, really. So why should he?

Because apathy was the new America.

The day still brutally hot, the sky still laden with hazy green smog. He saw pigeons, and doves, and sparrows; the ugly and obnoxious black great-tailed grackles. They soared gracefully in the sky.

A few blocks over, he heard the sirens of all the police cars, and all the ambulances, and the fire trucks still cleaning the bodies—the mess—of Lauro, the murdered kids.

"Is this the motherfucker right here?"

He felt the gun at his head.

Miss Padilla and her boyfriend stepped from the shadows of another abandoned house.

So fast, Angel didn't have time to notice them before it was too late and her boyfriend was behind Angel, pointing the gun.

"That's him," Miss Padilla said, "Fuckin' no good rotten kid."

From their doorway, Momma Rodriguez waved.

Looking to the sky, Angel saw the sun, the birds in the sky.

The boyfriend flashed a mouth full of gold, "Take back what's yours," he said.

Miss Padilla smiled, satisfied.

Then she snatched back the gold chains from Angel's hand.

He looked in his palm before the gun took his life, and he was holding Brandy's thin gold chain, the one she had hoped to pass to her daughter someday.

The Gleaner's Union

by Court Merrigan

I come home from the Gleaner's Union hangdog with a corn whiskey stumble in my step, trying not to believe what the boys was saying. How a man didn't hardly have a choice no more. How he had to hire out. The boys who still came in to the Union, they was stalwart, they knew good as me the difference between laboring for wages and working your own land. But young ones can't eat your knowing all winter, can they?

Cora sat by the stove, skinning spuds.

"How you been, little girl?" I said to her. "You go out walking today?"

"Yeah," she said.

She looked up from that half-skinned spud all ladylike, knees pressed tight together, hands on her lap. Cora never sat like that unless she was bad upset.

I pulled up a chair. Took the tater and knife out of Cora's slick little hands. Wanted to wrap her up in my big arms but that wouldn't do, big as she was getting.

"Ma," I said, "I plain forgot to change out the goat's hay. Maybe you want to give it a look."

"I already been out there," said Ma. I just..." Then she saw how I was looking at Cora. "Yeah," she said, reaching for her coat. "I better check."

She's always been a good woman.

"Now what is it, baby girl?" I said to Cora when Ma was gone.

"I was over round Griselda Harlan's place today," she said.

"Cora..."

"I know you told me and told me. But I didn't mean nothing by it. I was coming back out of Seven Mile Draw and you know that tree line they got's the best way to get back. It's out of the wind."

"Out of sight from the house, you mean."

Cora nodded. We'd all helped Harlan plant in that windbreak and of course them trees come up like weeds the first years before the drought and alkali. Now they was just thick tangles of branches for pheasants to hide out in.

"I seen Mr. Ryne and Griselda," said Cora.

"That's Mrs. Harlan to you, little girl."

"Him and Mrs. Harlan. I known it was Mr. Ryne because of that Mustang of his tied up outside."

"Go on."

"I saw em, Pa. Together."

"Together."

"I just wanted to see, Pa. I couldn't help myself."

Feature of life out there in that hardscrabble valley: no one had curtains. Couldn't afford em, for one thing, didn't need em, for another, what with your nearest neighbors living miles away.

"Well, what'd you see?" I asked.

"They was rutting, Pa."

She didn't have to say it, of course. Maybe I shouldn't of made her come out with it.

"Mrs. Harlan, she was bent over the table, and Mr. Ryne, his face was all twisted up and..."

"That'll do, girl," I said. "They see you?"

"No. They was too busy."

We sat there a while, pondering the possibilities.

"Pa," Cora said, "you can't go rutting someone you ain't married to, can you?"

"No, baby girl," I said, "you cannot."

*****

You want to go back, you'd blame it on Harlan's taking the job with the railroad. Course, he only took that job on account of the alkali eating up his land. For that you'd have to blame God. Or the government putting out the land around Spirit Lake, Wyoming, up for homesteading, what used to be Indian ground—but of course they never done nothing with it. Hundred-sixty acres free and clear if you pledged to work it seven years.

Course, we wasn't up here three years before the drought come on and never let go and the alkali started leaching up, poisoning the soil yellow so nothing would grow on it. Then you throw the Depression on top of that.

That's when we started finding out who was who. Some up and disappeared into the night, like them Okies down south jumping the Dust Bowl for California, giving up their land to get owned body and soul for a few bucks a day. Others kept their name on the deed and went out laboring, like Harlan.

Like I say, Harlan got on at the railroad. A good job, too, working the lines across the state two weeks at a stretch. A hundred men a day down at the rail yard clamoring for that job. We all thought Harlan got lucky till we heard he took his wife Griselda along with him. She was a looker, all right. Flouncing around in skirts and makeup like she lived downtown in Omaha or some such and not on parcel of hardscrabble Wyoming dirt a hundred miles from anywhere. You could see how a man could come by a job by her, if she got left alone with the hiring man a few minutes.

Issue 1

Harlan would be gone two, three weeks at a time. Not many women can cope with that kind of lonesomeness and Griselda wasn't one of em. So Jack Ryne come along to comfort her. Riding a fine Mustang, best horse in Spirit Lake.

*****

Cora now, you couldn't keep her to the homeplace if you strapped a plow to her back. I know we was sometimes the talk of folks, the way Cora would come strolling across someone's place chewing on a hickory stick in her boy's overalls, hair ragged short because she clipped it herself with sheep shears, toting along some Indian artifact she found back in the bluffs. Howdy doo, she'd say, have herself a drink of water out of the well and stroll on. I'd hear about it a couple days later and I know there was folks saying I should of reined her in.

But I couldn't do that. It was in Cora's blood. I remember our first harvest here, when times was still good. Cora just turned up down in the fields, right next to the reaper, pretty as you please. She wasn't but three years old. I held her on my lap as she grabbed at the chaff floating by, her thin hair smelling like wheat and everything in the world seeming open and possible. That was the fall of '28. Good times ain't been seen around here since.

Cora knows this country better than anyone since the Indians, I guess. The draws and the buttes beyond the farm ground, every plant and animal and bug and fish. How many times did she show me things I never knew existed: deer beds, trout eggs, seep draws, edible berries.

"What are these even called?" I asked her once.

"Hackberry."

"How did you know you could eat em?"

"I tried one."

"You could of got sick to death, girl. You can't go around eating things you don't know what they are."

She shrugged. "I know."

Being with Cora the world took on a wondering glow. I noticed cows had marvelously shaped noses, like she said, how ladybugs flitted like storybook fairies, ants dancing on the sand in the wind. You don't go restraining a creature like that. No sir.

*****

There wasn't no harvest that October of '36. Some of us had known since May, when didn't nothing come sprouting out of the alkali-killed ground. Some of us by July, when it hadn't rained in three months and Spirit Lake got too low to pull any more irrigation water out of. Some by September when three hailstorms in four days pounded the last living crops into dust and nothing. October should of been harvest. Instead them of us that hadn't run off to California or taken to laboring gathered at the Gleaner's Union warehouse that we built together, talking about what was and what might of been. Pass around corn whiskey, roll another smoke.

Cora had rode with me into the Union many and many a time during harvest back in the good days, sitting proud beside me on the seat. She'd grab a Coke out of the ice chest while we unloaded, prattling on to the bookkeeper Mrs. Rubottom about the critters and the clouds and the shape of the wind. Old Mrs. Rubottom nodding along as she kept track of the spuds and corn and wheat so we'd be sure to get our fair share at the end of harvest, each family proportioned to what it'd put in, sliding some of the profit over to families with newborns and sick ones, reckoning out payments on a tractor for everyone in the Union to share out.

Now Mrs. Rubottom was dead, there wasn't no call for bookkeeping, and I didn't tote Cora along to the

Union. Bunch of idled dirt farmers quaffing whiskey in a empty warehouse cussing at the world ain't no place for a little girl.

I had to walk in myself. The last horse on my team gave out in September after it drank alkali-poisoned water. I wasn't the only one walking, I'll tell you that. Them that still had horses were more lucky than good.

*****

A few days after me and Cora had our little talk, I was back at the Gleaner's Union. Whiskey jugs making the rounds, some of the boys talking about hiring out when Jerry Sherrill said to hell with that. He was headed into the mountains to trap bears. Said them pelts would bring fifty dollars or better down in Casper. But you couldn't walk the furs out. You needed a animal.

"You really think there's still bear back there?" I asked.

"I know there is," said Sherrill. "And wolf. Mink, even. They're begging for pelts down in Casper. You got them rich ladies out in New York paying top dollar, you know."

I thought about my dead team of horses. "Be damned," I said.

Ron Weizkowski come riding up. He'd brought along another jug. He joined in the jawing and allowed that if a man had four-legged transport, there was pelts for him up in the mountains.

"You'd need that good horse both ways, though," he said.

"You got a good horse," said Sherrill.

"She's all right," said Weizkowski, eyeing his mare. "But she don't hold no candle to that Mustang of Ryne's. I ought to know. I just seen it."

"Did you now?" I said.

"Over on Pumpkin Ridge," said Weizkowski. "Asked him if he didn't maybe want to join us. He said he had business elsewhere."

"I know where, the son of a bitch," I said.

*****

We called Ryne all the names, and Harlan all the names, and Griselda all the names. The jugs kept going around and we decided we best look into this ourselves. About half a dozen of us mounted up. We didn't have no plans. We hadn't got that far along. Them that didn't come cheered us as we left, holding up jugs in salute. I rode double with Weizkowski.

Righteousness kept us warm the seven-mile ride to Harlan's, wind blowing to beat a banshee. Harlan's place was scrimmed over in a year's worth of weeds. He hadn't put no crop in. Too busy getting owned for wages. Harlan's cur set to yapping and the front door swung open and there was Griselda Harlan standing in a square of light, hands on her hips. Looking disheveled in a pretty blue dress, the kind a woman wears when she plans on getting seen.

"Hello boys," she says to me. "Where you headed?"

They was all looking at me. I could tell if I didn't say what was needful, no one else would.

"Right here," I said.

She wasn't no kind of fighter, Griselda Harlan. She backed out of the entranceway leaving the door swung open and we piled in. Crowded in that front room where a couple gas lamps hissed. Good fire going in the stove. The table laid for two, glasses and china. Ryne was in there, all right. Eyes twitching like a trapped creature. He had on a clean shirt. The only man there whose shirt was.

"Hello fellas," Ryne said. "Looks like I wasn't the only one feeling neighborly this evening."

"Some more neighborly than others," I said.

Issue 1

Griselda bustled over to the stove, put on a kettle.

"You can leave off with the coffee," I said. "You know why we're here."

Griselda clanged down the kettle. I could see her hands shaking.

"We all got to look after one another," said Ryne.

Sherrill spit on the floor.

"Cut the shit," said Weizkowski.

"Hey now," said Ryne. "There's a lady here."

"Ain't no lady I can see," I said.

The room got quiet.

"Now boys," said Ryne, holding out his hands.

"You been fooling where you ain't ought to of been fooling," I said.

"We can't have it," said Weizkowski.

"Hell, boys," said Ryne, "it ain't what you think."

"No, it's worse," I said. "Ain't it, Griselda?"

Griselda looked at Ryne to say something else but he never did. He ran.

He crashed out of the back bedroom window, screeching like a little girl. We got turned around, banging into one another and back out the front door, Griselda's china smashed to the floor.

Like I say, it was a year's worth of weeds out there. Out back of the house they was tall as a man. That and we was half-cocked, in no kind of condition to go tracking in the dark. We might of gave up the whole business but for who stepped out of the weeds.

Cora.

"This way, Pa!" she said. "Come on!"

Wasn't nothing for it but to do like she said. We followed her over the cracked alkali ground. She knew the lay of the land but good. Ran us right up the little draw where Ryne was trying to make a hidey hole out of a fox den.

Things might of gone different for him if he hadn't run, so that a ten-year old girl had to smoke him out for us. Now our blood was up. We glugged down the rest of that whiskey and yanked his trousers down and took out a sharp knife. Held Griselda, made her watch, sobbing. After, I saw Harlan's cur loping away into the night with Ryne's manhood.

*****

Cora, she hung tight to me the whole ride home. Six miles over the hills, cold wind cutting us all the way. First couple miles, didn't neither of us say nothing.

"He going to live, Pa?" Cora finally asked.

"Not well. But he ain't going to die, if that's what you mean." We rode on a ways. "You understand, don't you?" I asked.

"You can't go rutting someone you ain't married to," Cora said.

"That's right."

"I like this horse, Pa."

"He's a good one, all right."

That Mustang was, too. He'd ride me right up into the mountains and carry the furs out. Keep me off the wages. Cora behind me patted the Mustang's shanks.

"You going to take me up with you after the bears?" she asked.

"How'd you know about that?" I said.

She shrugged. "I know."

Magpie
by Hilary Davidson

The sheriff who called about my mother-in-law's death sounded genuinely sad about it. "She looked like she was called up to the Lord all peaceful-like," he said, in a deep voice that had a lingering drawl to it. "She went in her sleep, I reckon. I'm sure she didn't feel no pain."

He told me that she'd died of a heart attack, and that it had probably happened a couple of days earlier, given the state in which she was found. "Couple of her near neighbors hadn't seen her about, so they went over, and then they called me. Poor Mrs. Carlow. Let me give you my number so your husband can call me."

I dutifully wrote it down, then folded the paper and put it into my purse. It was just before noon, and Jake was probably with a patient, maybe even in surgery. Telling him the news about his mother over the phone seemed heartless. I could drive to his office and reveal all in person, but given that he hadn't spoken to his mother in years, that seemed like overkill. The news could wait until evening, after he got home. There wasn't anything either of us could do about it now. His mother had lived in the western edge of Ohio, close to the border with West Virginia. Jake and I were in Los Angeles, where we'd moved for his medical practice. We'd been there almost five years, and even though his roots were in hill country and mine were in Cleveland, the West Coast felt completely like home.

Jake surprised me an hour later, the tires of his Porsche squealing into the driveway. I met him at the door.

"My mother's dead," he said. We clung to each other for a while.

"I'm sorry, baby."

"Ludy said they think she died in her sleep."

"Ludy?" I pulled back. "You talked to your sister?"

"She called to tell me what happened."

"She called your office?" My stomach suddenly clenched into knots. "How did she…"

"Never mind that now, Erica. I need to think." He pushed me away and headed for his den, slamming the door behind him. I was too surprised to say anything, or to go after him. He didn't seem sad so much as unsettled. That wasn't a surprise: it was normal to mourn a parent, even one who was a mean, manipulative person. Jake had cut off contact with her years ago because of her abusiveness, and while he was right to do it, I suspected that his conscience wasn't easy right now. Any sense of loss would be made worse if it was accompanied by guilt.

When I knocked on the door, he didn't answer. I listened at it for a moment, but all was quiet. He had alcohol in there, I knew, but no food, so I went to the kitchen and made him a sandwich. I put it on a tray and wrote a little note on an index card—I love you, baby—and left it in front of the door, knocking to let him know it was there. An hour later, it was untouched, like a rejected peace offering at the altar of an angry god.

That was when I started to worry. My husband was a man with a tender heart; he found it hard to hold a grudge against anyone, no matter how deserving. It had been so painful for him to cut off contact with his mother, even though he'd done so for reasons any sane person would understand. You couldn't put up with a toxic person just because you were related to her; you still had to draw a line somewhere. Mrs. Carlow had actually made it easier for

Jake by ignoring him. Jake had sent her a birthday card once, after they cut off contact. I only knew about it because his mother had crossed out her name with a spidery X and wrote RETURN TO SENDER on the envelope, so the card boomeranged back. How did you mourn a mother like that?

I wandered aimlessly through our house, wondering what to do. Jake needed help, but I wasn't sure how to give it to him. We'd been together for a dozen years, and yet sometimes I found it hard to understand him.

When I knocked again on the door of his study, he ignored me. But he hadn't locked me out, and the knob turned under my hand. I stepped over the tray and went inside. The blinds were drawn, but I could see Jake's silhouette at his desk. He seemed to be staring into space. I didn't hear the music at first, it was turned so low. The lyrics came as a whisper: *"Oh, Death, oh death, please spare me over till another year."*

"What is it, Erica?" Jake's voice was just as quiet as the singer's.

I'd prepared a speech in my mind, but it slipped away. "I'm sorry," I blurted out. "I wish I knew what to do to help you, baby."

Jake just looked at me with that hard, flat expression that came over him when he got lost inside his own thoughts. Normally, I could cajole him out of it, but I had a feeling that I wouldn't be able to this time. He was too bitter and raw right now. He was dangerous at the moment, liable to do something rash if I didn't pay very close attention to him.

"There's nothing anyone can do now. What's done is done."

"It's normal to have conflicted feelings in a situation like this. It's…"

"Erica, please cut out the bullshit psychobabble. I can't listen to it now."

That made a lump swell in my throat. Jake almost never cursed, certainly not at me. He was more depressed than I'd realized.

"I have to go out there," he muttered.

"You what?"

"I need to go home for my mother's funeral."

"Jake, she's gone and nothing is going to change that. Going to her funeral isn't going to help her. It's just going to drag you back to a place you hate and bring back painful memories."

"I'd rather have the painful memories than whitewash the past."

"You're so busy at work," I pointed out. "They need you at the clinic. You can't just leave them in the lurch."

"Why? Because some starlet wouldn't get her boob job? Or maybe some spoiled teenager wouldn't get her bumpy nose fixed?"

"You're picking ridiculous examples. You know you do wonderful work. Important work. Think of all the little kids you've helped." Jake occasionally spent his weekends performing surgery, for free, on poor kids from the inner city whose parents could never have afforded to fix their cleft palates and other disfigurements.

He rubbed his temples. "It's not enough."

"Look, let's make a donation in your mother's honor. I was looking online, and there's this one association that focuses on heart attack and stroke prevention for women."

Jake stared at me for what felt like a very long time. "How did you know my mother died of a heart attack?"

"Oh, I…" I felt terrible for not telling him about the sheriff's call sooner. But when he'd come home, he'd already known that his mother was dead, and he'd disappeared into his den before I'd had the chance to say anything. "The sheriff who found her called here, right before you came in. I was going to call you, but then I was thinking I should tell you in person, and then you came home and you already knew…"

He put his hand up. "I don't want to hear it. Just leave me alone."

I swallowed hard and backed out of the room. "Let me know if you need anything," I said, pulling the door behind me. Just before it closed, I stopped and poked my head back in the room. "I love you, baby."

Jake just stared at me. I shut the door and tried not to panic.

*****

Jake surprised me late that night, leaving his den and joining me in bed. He didn't want comfort or sleep. He wanted me. Maybe that was the only way he could forget his pain. By the time he was done, our sheets were sticky with lust and sweat, and I fell asleep in his arms, feeling at peace with the world.

In the morning, I woke up alone. Jake's gym bag was gone, and I thought he'd gone to the club early to play squash. I was glad, because I thought that was a sign Jake had turned a corner, that the crisis I'd felt was impending was going to be averted.

But then I realized Jake's laptop was gone. Sitting in its place on his desk was a white sheet from a company that made some sort of line-filling injectable gel.

I had to go home, it read.

I crumpled it into a ball and threw it against the wall. Home? He still thought of that hellhole in the sticks as home? That turned my stomach. What about our home together? What about our life together? I picked up the phone, looked at the numbers Jake had called recently, and hit redial. What did he think he was doing? Was he determined to ruin his life? Jake could be impulsive, acting first and worrying about consequences later. I had to save him from himself.

*****

In theory, I knew where I was going. I got on a red-eye flight that night that took me from Los Angeles to Charlotte, and then a connecting flight on a commuter plane to Charleston, West Virginia. It was easy enough to rent a car and follow the highway west, to where it ran alongside the Ohio River, but once I crossed the bridge, I was on my own. Google Maps could only take me so far through the barren, miserable wilderness of hill country.

Jake had taken me to visit his family there only once, just before we got married. We'd been engaged forever, and he was close to finishing his medical residency. "I can't marry a girl my family hasn't met," he told me. That settled it.

"They're not going to like me," I warned him. "They're going to see me as some city snob in high heels."

"They'll love you," Jake soothed me. "They already know how smart and hard-working you are. That you were a scholarship student like I was. They know you were raised by your mom, and that she died when you were in high school."

"You told them that?"

"It's nothing to be ashamed of, Erica. You should be proud that you started with nothing and worked hard to get where you are."

"What else did you tell them about me?" I seethed.

"Everything that's wonderful about you," he said, kissing me. "And I want you to see how wonderful it is there. You're going to love it."

I knew he was wrong about that, but I didn't have the heart to tell him. I'd worked hard to break free from government housing and food stamps, and I hadn't done that so I could live in a mountain shack. I had other plans.

The visit went just as badly as I knew it would. "Didn't think I'd be seeing you 'round here. Ain't you able to come up with some excuse not to darken my doorstep?" Those were the first words out of Mrs. Carlow's mouth when she saw us at the door. Jake, being his usual sweet self, mollified her. But she fixed her narrow blue eyes on me and pursed her lips, looking me up and down. Sometimes, when people met me, they told me I looked exotic and used that as cover to ask about my race. Mrs. Carlow didn't ask that, but I felt those cold eyes parsing pieces out, not liking any of them. While Jake was able to thaw her out, she remained cold and rude with me. She didn't come out and say anything directly. Her insults were carefully couched in statements that were hard to answer.

"Them's some fine clothes you have," she'd told me. "What's that old saw? Fine feathers make fine birds?" She turned to Jake. "Cousin Hark's wife just walked out on him. She was one who always thought real well of herself." Her expression made it clear what she thought of women who thought well of themselves.

I knew, even then, that Mrs. Carlow believed she could chase me off. What she hadn't realized was that I'd already made up my mind about Jake and my own future, and that there wasn't a damn thing she could do about it. What she couldn't have realized was how much I wanted her to hate me.

I was thinking of that visit as I steered my rental car along the roads. Nature was something I loved in healthy doses. Being surrounded by hills and fields with no indications of people nearby—except for occasional tractor-crossing signs—made me nervous. When it got to be too much for me, I stopped the car and turned on my cell phone. Jake had tried to call me several times before I'd boarded my flight; I hadn't answered, and once I'd turned off my phone I hadn't turned it back on. He had to be sweating by now, wondering why I wasn't answering. I dialed his number and he answered immediately. "Why haven't you been answering your phone? I've been worried sick about you."

"Why did you go running off in the middle of the night? Why didn't you tell me?"

He sighed. "I knew if I did, I'd never get here. I just had to do it then, Erica. It was important. Don't be upset, okay?"

"Oh, I'm upset all right. Especially because I'm sitting in the middle of nowhere trying to figure out how to get to where you are."

It took him a second to absorb that. "You flew out here? To be with me?"

"You didn't think I was just going to wait at home for you, did you, baby?"

"I was worried you'd be so angry you might file for divorce," he admitted in a sheepish tone.

"I'd never do that to you, baby," I said, and I meant it.

*****

The only person who seemed distinctly unhappy to see me was Kady. When Jake brought me back to her house, where all of the family was meeting, her mouth pursed, just like her mother's had when she'd met me. Kady had been friendly enough when I'd encountered her before, but now I saw bitterness and recrimination in her eyes. But that might only have heated up after her husband, a ruggedly handsome man named Ry, hugged me for longer than was strictly necessary.

"I'm sorry about your mother," I told her. She nodded, keeping her eyes on my face. Her own was red and blotchy, and her eyes were swollen. Her two young sons stopped running around long enough to inspect me, then took off, laughing. In the living room, a collection of cousins sat around drinking and laughing. It didn't seem as if anyone missed Mrs. Carlow much.

"You got here in a hurry," Kady said to me.

"It's a tough time for Jake. I wasn't going to leave him alone."

"You sure that's the reason? Or were you afraid he'd come back here and go native?" Kady's voice was more refined and less country than her mother's had been, but it had the same twangy undertones.

"Go native?"

"You know exactly what I mean. You're the reason he never came home. Jake was going to come back and be a doctor here. You wouldn't let him do that."

"That's ridiculous. Jake never wanted to come back here."

"Yes, he did, and you're the one who ruined it. You're the one who got him to throw his life away, doing them plastic surgeries instead of proper medicine." As her temper heated up, her diction slipped.

"Last time I checked, Jake was an adult who could make his own decisions."

"You're a thief, nothing more."

"Really?" I rolled my eyes. "That was what your mother said, too. That was why Jake stopped speaking to her, you know."

"Oh, I know that full well. You got a hell of a nerve coming back here. You stole Mama's earrings just like she said you did. You're a thief and a liar."

"I didn't steal anything," I said, my voice calm. I had the truth on my side. Maybe I had told Jake a lie or two for his own good, but I'd never stolen anything.

"Mama caught you in her room that time Jake brought you to her house!"

"I just wanted to see the photographs. There was nothing wrong with that."

"Then she found her pearl earrings were gone. You took them. It had to be you."

"She went and grabbed my purse and dumped it out on the table because she thought they were in there," I said. "Then, when she found they weren't, she practically ripped off my blouse because she thought I was hiding them in my bra. She was wrong."

"You had them," Kady insisted. "You know what Mama called you? Magpie, on account of you seeing something good and shiny and not being able to keep yourself from thieving."

The insult rankled, but I wasn't going to let that show. "Your mother was delusional. Maybe that runs in the family."

"I don't know how you got them earrings outta the house, but you did. You stole them, sure as you stole my brother away from his home. But you're in for a surprise, because this time Jake's gonna stay where he belongs."

"You go on thinking that if it makes you happy," I said. "But after the funeral, we're going home."

*****

Jake and I went to his mother's house the next day. It was only my second time there, but I remembered it well. It was old-lady fussy, with plastic over the sofa and white doilies on the tables. There were little carvings and statuettes on every available surface, including a series of owls that were downright spooky.

"I'm surprised you were willing to come along for this, but I'm glad you did, Erica."

"I couldn't let you go through your mother's things by yourself, baby. That would be too stressful."

"Kady's already done a lot of the work. I'm just looking for anything I want to keep. Kady's already got the photo albums and Mama's jewelry and the family Bible at her place."

"Wow. She lost no time helping herself to your mother's things."

"Don't start, Erica. Please. This is stressful enough."

I bit my tongue. The last thing I needed to do was fight with Jake right now. I noticed his verbal lapse— Mama—and that made me nervous. Old habits came back quickly, didn't they? But I was also slightly annoyed with myself. Of course Kady took her mother's jewelry. If I'd planned ahead, I would have gotten a pair of earrings like

Issue 1

Mrs. Carlow had owned—baroque pearls on 14-karat gold stems—and set them in her jewelry box, then remarked on them while Jake was nearby. It was too late for that now. Better to stick with my original plan.

While Jake was going through the record collection, I slipped out of my dress. For a moment I debated leaving my bra and panties on and letting Jake remove them, but then I pulled them off, too. It was important not to have any margin for error. I went up behind him and wrapped my arms around his waist from behind.

"This isn't a good time, Erica. I can't right now."

"Oh, baby, you always can."

We went back and forth like that for a while. I thought he might give in, but all of those owls watching had a negative effect on his libido. After a while I sighed and said I was going to the bathroom.

"You'll keep an eye on my purse and stuff, right?" I called from the doorway.

Jake turned. It was important that he know I was completely naked. "Sure. But no one's running off with it."

I went to the bathroom and closed the door. Everything in the room was pink or had a floral print on it. There was even a pink owl sitting next to the sink.. It made me feel a little self-conscious as I knelt down and opened the vanity. Inside were half-used bottles of shampoo, boxes of baking soda, and other junk I didn't care about. Instead, I ran my fingers along the inside ledge just above the doors. When I hit something that felt like hardened putty, I pried it loose. There, encased in hardened gum, were the missing earrings, just as I'd left them. When I pried them free, I noticed that the pearls were looking a little gray. Of course, pearls needed contact with skin to keep their luster. These had been neglected for five years.

"You won't believe what I found," I told Jake when I came out. I put the earrings into his hand.

"Where did you get these?"

"They were in the bathroom."

"They've been in the house all this time?" He frowned. "Where were they, exactly?"

"In the medicine cabinet."

"Why were you in the medicine cabinet?"

"Why does that matter? I was looking for a Band-Aid, okay?" This wasn't the reaction I'd expected at all. "The point is, your mother accused me of stealing her earrings, and they've been here all this time."

"I don't think these are the same ones. They look fake."

"If they're fake, it's because they were always fake!" I was exasperated. "Those are the earrings."

"How can you be sure?"

I stopped, realizing that that was a trick question. That time we'd visited, I'd denied even seeing the earrings. How could I claim I knew what they looked like. "I guess I just got excited when I saw them. Like maybe your mother realized she was wrong." I started to get dressed. I'd wanted Jake to know that I hadn't carried anything into the bathroom with me, but now that seemed pointless.

"I'll give them to Kady. She'll know them better than me."

But Kady wasn't any more convinced than her brother when she saw them. "These look like cheap-ass imitations. Not the real thing," she said.

They did look like fakes, truth be told. But that wasn't my fault.

"You think they're Mama's?" Jake asked.

"I'd bet they're replacements put there by someone with a guilty conscience." Kady looked at me. I fought the urge to kick her and turned to the window. Her husband, Ry, was outside, playing with their boys. This trip wasn't going as I expected it to at all. I needed to do something to fix that fast, before it was too late.

*****

"We need to talk," Jake told me on the morning of his mother's funeral.

"What is it, baby?"

"We've been out in Los Angeles for five years. I'm not happy there. I don't like the work I'm doing. I trained as an otolaryngologist, and what am I doing? I'm making starlets look like Barbie."

"But you're doing so well. They love you at the clinic. And every month you volunteer…"

"It's not enough, Erica. I want to help people here. That was always my plan. I just got sidetracked."

"Sidetracked?" I stared at him. "You have a great life. These people here, don't you think any of them would kill to get what you have? You got out. That's what the people here want to do."

"It's not like your old neighborhood, Erica. There are a lot of people happy to be living out here. I'm sick of being in the city."

"This is just guilt talking," I said. "Your mother died, and now you feel bad. Never mind that she was an evil person who told lies about people to try to manipulate you."

"Erica." He looked at me, his face serious. "That time we visited her…you didn't accidentally take her earrings or anything like that, did you?"

"I can't believe you're even asking." Now I was getting angry. "I told you then, and I can't believe you're making me say it again, but I swear to you, I didn't steal her earrings, accidentally or otherwise."

"It's just… it's kind of funny you found those replacements. It is a little weird."

"I guess your whole family thinks I'm a thief and a liar."

"Of course not, Erica. I'm sorry, I just…"

I walked out of the room. We were silent on the drive to the church; at least, I was. Jake made a few attempts at conversation, which I ignored. At the church, I sat next to him, but stared straight ahead, ignoring him. Jake was busy consoling Kady, who wore a frumpy black dress and a big black hat with a veil. The two of them stood over their mother's casket for the longest time.

"Can't say I miss the old bat," Kady's husband, Ry, whispered to me. "She was a pain in the ass. She was always fighting with somebody."

I'd thought to pack a form-fitting black designer dress that hugged my curves. Jake was too preoccupied to notice, but it didn't escape Ry.

Back at the house for the wake, Ry whispered, "So, Kady says you planted fake pearls at her mama's house. She's all steamed about it."

"What makes you think I did something?" I smiled at him.

He grinned back. "You're the kinda gal who's always up to something, Erica."

"Well, it's never good to be boring." We clinked glasses. Ry was drinking bourbon, while I was guzzling more wine than I'd planned. It was frustrating, knowing I was right about something and not being able to prove it.

"It must've been awful, living only an hour away from Mrs. Carlow," I said.

"Lemme tell you about that." He did, and he made me laugh, which earned some dark looks from Kady. Then Ry followed me when I went upstairs.

"Don't think I didn't notice you staring at me," I said. We were standing in the guest bedroom where Jake and I were staying. I looked in the mirror and unpinned my hair.

"Don't think I didn't notice you enjoying it," he answered.

"Do you think anyone will come up here?"

"Not if we're quiet."

I pounced on him. Ry was a surprisingly good kisser. I thought about Kady's sour face and figured he must be getting practice somewhere else. He started to unzip my dress. "No," I whispered. "Rip it off."

"But it must've cost a pretty penny."

"Rip it off," I ordered. There was a sound like a series of pops as the fabric broke apart at the seam.

"Oh, I like this," Ry said.

"I bet you do." With that, I reached out and raked my nails over his face.

"What the fuck?" He pushed me away and touched his skin. I let out a bloodcurdling scream, opened the door, and ran from the room. Jake was on the stairs and I ran into his arms. Then I sobbed and sobbed.

*****

The trip home to Los Angeles was uneventful. Jake was silent most of the time. I wore a little eye mask so that I could sleep, but occasionally I would tug at the corner to watch him. He was drinking whiskey, his jaw taut. Every so often his eyes would narrow, but mostly he just drank.

"Do you think I did the right thing?" I asked him. "By not pressing charges against Ry, I mean."

"I think that would've been a mistake," Jake answered. "Those kids don't need their dad locked up in jail."

"At long as he doesn't attack some other woman," I mused.

"He won't do that," Jake muttered.

That made me frown, but he didn't say anything else and I let the matter drop. I fell asleep somewhere over the Midwest, and when I did, I dreamt I was back in Mrs. Carlow's house.

"What are you doing in here?" she snapped at me, just as she had in real life. I was in her bedroom, standing in front of her dresser. There were framed photos there, of her dead husband and her children, and one of Mrs. Carlow herself before she was Mrs. anything.

"Nothing," I said, brushing past her and walking down the hall, turning into the bathroom. My heart was racing as I locked the door. I opened my hand and saw the earrings in my palm. There was a beautiful black bird sitting in the open window, and I dropped the pearls into her mouth. Then magpie flew away until she was just a distant dot on the horizon, getting as far from that place as fast as she could.

Lady Madeline's Dive

by Terrence P. McCauley

NEW YORK CITY
1928

Quinn's mouth went dry when he saw the green and white squad car in his rearview mirror. The red spotlight flashing, but no siren.

Normally, getting pulled over by the cops was a simple inconvenience. Most of them were on Archie Doyle's payroll anyway. Just like Quinn.

But that night was different. Because the Plymouth that he was driving was stolen.

And there was a dead man in the trunk.

Dead men in trunks of stolen cars and cops don't mix. Even cops on the take have limits on what they'll ignore. This wasn't Chicago; it was New York.

He thought about taking a hard right turn and flooring it; disappearing into traffic. He might've even gotten away. But he decided to try talking his way out of it instead. He took his foot off the gas and eased the Plymouth over toward the right side of Houston Street.

He was surprised when the squad car sped past him heading west. They hadn't been looking to pull him over after all. They'd just wanted him to get out of their way.

The cop in the passenger seat leaned out the window and gave him a big wave. A beat cop named O'Hara—one of Archie's boys from before they passed Volstead eight years prior. Quinn waved back and began to breathe again.

At the next red light, he lit a cigarette and drew the smoke deep into his lungs. The tobacco revved his nerves and gave him the kick he needed to stay awake. He needed all the help he could get.

He felt dried out and hungover, like he was on the fifth day of a four-day bender. It wasn't from too much booze or too many late nights on the town. It was from a lack of sleep, courtesy of the dead bastard in the trunk.

It had all started a few days before, when Doyle had realized the take from one of his gambling dives had been short—very short—every week for the past month. Doyle hadn't told Quinn how short, but short enough to get Doyle's attention.

And short enough for him to ask Quinn to find out why.

The dive was off an alley on 14th Street run by Lady Madeline and her husband, a hophead named Joey. The place was a pit, but it had always made good coin. Lady Madeline and Joey had never had problems making Doyle's payments before.

So Doyle had Quinn do some digging. He checked around and found out that the place was busier than ever, especially since Doyle gave them the okay to start selling booze. His booze, of course. The take being off meant someone was getting greedy. And stupid.

People didn't steal from Doyle very often, but when they did, it was up to Quinn to find out why and to put a stop to it. One way or the other.

Hence the dead guy in the trunk.

Issue 1

Quinn hadn't meant to kill him. If the little son of a bitch had kicked loose with the information earlier, he would've still been alive. Instead, the man decided to play it tough. It took Quinn almost two nights to break him, and in the end the little punk died anyway. A bum heart. A bad break.

Normally, Archie would've let him dump the body somewhere public, a place where someone would find him. Word would hit the street even before the cops showed up to remove the body. The story would've run in all the papers and the message would've been loud and clear: Steal from Archie Doyle and see what happens.

Example made. Problem solved.

But this time, Archie didn't just want to solve a problem. This time, he wanted to make a statement that would show the other Lady Madelines and Joeys in Doyle's empire what happens to people who steal from him.

And it was up to Quinn to make that statement loud and clear.

Quinn hated statements. Because statements had a way of getting awfully complicated awfully fast, especially where dead bodies were involved.

Complicated as in a random car stop by the cops in the middle of the night.

Quinn didn't like it, but Doyle didn't ask his opinion. Doyle paid him to do what he was told and that's exactly what he was going to do. Archie wanted to make a statement and Quinn was going to see that he did.

Loud and clear.

Tonight.

*****

He parked the Plymouth across the street from Lady Madeline's and left it there. He tossed the keys down by the pedals, like they'd simply dropped out of someone's pocket.

His watch told him it was a bit after one in the morning. He craved sleep, but he still had work to do.

He put half a block between him and the Plymouth and spent the next half-hour in a doorway, chain-smoking while he eyeballed the alley leading to Lady M's joint across the street. At a few inches over six feet tall and two hundred pounds, Quinn stood out in a crowd, but the doorway was a good spot: just enough shadow to keep anyone from seeing him while he waited for his signal to come over.

As big as he was, he never walked into a place without looking it over first. Especially a two-bit clip-joint like Lady M's.

The scene matched what he'd been told. Foot traffic in and out of the alley was heavy—too heavy for a place on the downswing. Too heavy for Lady M's tribute to Doyle to be so light.

It was almost one-thirty when he saw Otis Rae, the dive's piano player, come outside and light a cigarette at the curb.

That was the cue he'd been waiting for.

He pushed his fatigue aside. Time to go to work.

He jogged through traffic against the light as he crossed the street. Some cars stopped short, but no one cursed at him. No one honked their horn, either.

Because you just didn't honk at Terry Quinn.

Otis shook his head as he reached the sidewalk. At 5'3", the Negro was a foot shorter than Quinn, but had a heavyweight's attitude.

"After all the shit you been through," Otis said, "that's how you'll die. Flattened by a Studebaker in front of a shithouse like this."

"Next time I'll wait for you to come carry me across."

Otis took a deep drag on his cigarette. "Be a long goddamned wait 'fore that happens."

Quinn nodded back to ward the alley. "Looks like you're doing some business. Hell of a crowd from what I've seen."

"No different than any other night lately." Otis looked around before saying, "Glad your boss finally got wise to that."

Otis had been the first one Quinn had called when Doyle realized his take was off. And Otis confirmed business had been good and steady. "Archie appreciates your loyalty. He won't forget it."

Otis shrugged. "Just don't go bustin' up my piano while you're in there. A man's gotta make a livin' and that piano's my livin'."

"This is just a social call. No rough stuff, I promise."

Otis looked him up and down. "Your social calls got a way of gettin' awfully un-social pretty goddamned fast."

Quinn broke into a full-blown smile. The piano player knew him too well. "Madeline back in her office?"

Otis nodded. "That's why I signaled you to come over. And she ain't alone, neither."

"That so? Joey with her?"

Otis shook his head. "Haven't seen him for three days or more, but she's got some gentlemen callers back there with her tonight. Couple of society fellas by the looks of 'em. White boys in tuxedos. Stiff collars and soft bellies. You know the type."

He did. "Anyone else?"

"A boy named Carmine. Don't know his last name, but he's one of Howard Rothmann's boys. Been hangin' round here with Madeline and Joey on and off for the past month or so."

Quinn knew all about Carmine. His last name was Rizzo and he was smart and tough. A rare combination for a Rothmann goon.

Quinn tucked a twenty into the piano player's shirt pocket as he headed down the alley. "Thanks, Otis. I'll be gentle as a lamb, I promise."

Otis grunted as he flicked the ash from his cigarette into the gutter. "Where've I heard that one before?"

*****

The doormen saw Quinn coming and stood aside.

Lady Madeline's dive was a gambling joint first and foremost and had never tried to be anything else. Bare floors and bare walls. Chipped paint and dim lighting. Uneven wooden floors that popped and groaned beneath his feet as he walked inside.

The place hummed with busy gambling sounds. Murmurs and cheers and groans. The sounds of chips clicking and dice tumbling and the roulette ball skipping along the grooves of the wheel. The air was humid with stale smoke and sweat.

Otis's upright piano was against the far wall and was usually played when the place got quiet, which wasn't too often. The pit bosses doubled as bouncers and kept their eyes on everyone and everything. The tables, the gamblers and, of course, the money. Always the money. The bosses all knew Quinn and knew enough to leave him alone.

Every inch of the place was dedicated to gambling—blackjack, poker, roulette, craps. And every table had dozens of eager gamblers crowded around, waiting for a spot to open up. Waiting for Lady Luck to come whisper in their ear.

The place didn't have a proper bar because all of Doyle's gambling dens had a motto: No bar, no bullshit. Just gambling. Lady M's was one of the few places in Doyle's operation where you could get a drink if you were at one of the tables. And even then, one of the girls went to the back and got it for you.

If you weren't gambling, you weren't drinking. Simple as that. And if you got too sloppy, you got cut off and thrown out. If you complained, you were never allowed to come back. It kept the nonsense down to a minimum, which kept the cops happy.

Quinn edged his way through the crowd of gamblers, toward the back room that Lady Madeline called her office. He didn't have to push too hard. Everyone saw him coming and edged out of his way.

He was surprised to find the door wasn't locked. He pushed it in and found himself in the middle of a party.

Madeline was lounging on her couch with a glass of champagne, her boozy cackle filling the small room. She was surrounded by the three men Otis had described— two boys in tuxedoes on her left and Carmine Rizzo seated on her right. Carmine's back was to the wall.

They all stopped laughing when they saw Terry Quinn was standing in the doorway.

Rizzo looked more alert than scared and kept his hands on his lap. In plain sight and no sudden movements. Carmine was a smart boy indeed.

The other two in the tuxes weren't so smart. Quinn judged them both to be in their early twenties and of the well-bred, over-fed variety. Big on money and short on sense.

The one on the couch next to Lady M was the smaller of the two. Skinnier and blonder than his friend, with pink skin and scared blue eyes that darted back and forth between Quinn and Lady M.

But the other tux wasn't so docile. He slowly got up from his chair and, judging by the way he was swaying, he was more than a bit drunk. He was a broad, dark-haired kid with mean, reckless eyes. Quinn pegged him as a prep school bully who'd been a tough guy at Yale or Princeton. But there was softness about him, a softness that only a life of money could bring.

A softness Quinn had never had.

One of Lady M's loud, boozy snickers broke the tension. She was twenty years past pretty and had never been much of a looker to begin with. Her face and skin had the ruddy tinge that comes from too many years of too much gin and not enough sunlight. She was wearing a slinky black cocktail dress that a thin young woman would've had trouble wearing well. Lady M was neither thin nor young and hadn't been either for a very long time.

"Well, well, well," she cackled, "if it ain't my old pal Quinn." She slapped Rizzo on the knee. "You know who Terry Quinn is, don't you, Carmine?"

"Sure." Carmine's hands were still flat on his lap. "Everybody knows him. How's every little thing, Terry?"

"No complaints. You're a little far west, aren't you, Carmine? Last I checked, Rothmann's territory ends at Fifth Avenue."

Carmine made a show of straightening his tie. "I like to get out once in a while." He tried a smile. "See a better class of people."

Quinn smiled too. "Then what are you doing here?"

Lady M was drunk enough to laugh like that was the funniest thing since Prohibition. She drained her champagne glass, then held it out for Blondie to refill it. The kid couldn't stop looking at Quinn and damn near knocked over the bottle while he reached for it.

His big friend still stood there, breathing heavy and swaying while he tried to stare Quinn down. And Quinn kept on ignoring him.

Lady M smiled at the sound of the champagne filling her glass. "So how's about tellin' me what brings out Doyle's Black Hand into my humble abode this fine evening?"

"Business. We need to talk, Mimi."

"So talk!" Lady M threw open her arms in a grand gesture. "We're all friends here, ain't we boys?" She looked at Rizzo. "Carmine knows all about our kind of business, don't you Carmine?" She looked at the two boys in tuxedoes. "And these dapper gentlemen here…"

The big boy in the tux cut her off, "…don't know who the fuck you are, mister. We were having a damned swell party for ourselves before you showed up. So why don't you do yourself a favor and take it on the heel and toe so we can get back to our good time?"

He shuffled one step too close.

Quinn dropped him with a short left hook to the jaw. The blueblood fell back over his chair and hit the floor head first.

Carmine didn't move a muscle.

"That ain't nice, Terry," Madeline slurred. "That young man just so happens to be Jack Van Dorn of the Fifth Avenue Van Dorns."

"Then he should've been smart enough to keep his goddamned mouth shut. We've got business, Mimi. You and me. Alone. Right now."

Madeline's fleshy arms flapped as she threw up her hands and motioned for Blondie and Carmine to leave. Carmine moved first, slow and steady as he passed Quinn and out the door.

Blondie got to his feet and seemed to think about helping his friend, but ran out of the room instead. He even closed the door behind him. A nice, polite boy.

Quinn kept standing where he was.

Madeline drained her champagne glass again and filled it for herself. "You happy now, you goddamned animal? And stop callin' me Mimi in my own joint."

"It's Archie's joint. You and that shitbird husband of yours just run it for him. You'd do well to remember that."

"Archie Doyle," Mimi said, drawing out his name. "Joe and me have been runnin' this dive for three years and ain't never heard a word of complaint outta him before."

"That's because you never stole from him before."

"Stole?" Mimi lowered her champagne glass very slowly. If he didn't know better, he would've thought she was genuinely insulted. "Stole?" Her ruddy skin blanched quickly. "We stole? From Archie? Me and Joey? That what he tell you? After all we done for that miserable Irish son of a..."

"Stow the bullshit. Archie's take from this place has been off every week for the past month and it's not because business is off. You're leaking money, Mimi, and that means either you or Joe are getting greedy. Which one of you is it?"

Mimi sat up as straight as she could manage. "Neither me nor Joey ever stole off nobody, especially Archie. We run a gamblin' joint for Chrissakes! We make plenty off what we take in, even with Archie gettin' his cut."

"The take says different." He remembered Doyle's instructions. "If it's not you, it's got to be Joey. Where is he?"

"How the hell should I know," she said. "I ain't seen him for three whole days, the bum. Never could rely on that lousy bastard for nothin'."

"That's too bad. That just leaves you, unless someone else in this place was in on the skim with you. And the quicker you start talking, the easier this is going to be. For both of us."

Mimi shook a long, crooked finger at him. "Let me ask you somethin', tough guy. In all of this big thinkin' Archie's been doin', did the grand man himself ever ask why we'd steal from him? Now? After all these years, *now* we get greedy?"

"People change," he said. "Crazy notions pop into their heads out of nowhere. Notions like maybe they ought to jump ship and join up with Rothmann's bunch."

"Pshaw," she said with a boozy wave. "That's crazy talk."

"Not really." He nodded over at the chair where Carmine Rizzo had been sitting. "You having one of Rothmann's top boys in here tonight doesn't look too good."

Mimi's face became all lines and shadows. "First you call me a thief, then you call me a traitor. You sure know how to make a girl sore. You…"

"Quit stalling. I know damned well you've got the money you owe Archie with you right here and now. Just hand it over and Archie promises he'll forgive the whole thing for old time's sake. But if you keep lying to me, and I have to tear this place apart looking for it, things will get real ugly real fast."

He heard a floorboard creak behind him just before he heard the door open. He had plenty of time to go for his gun, but didn't.

Archie had already told him no gunplay.

Quinn heard the hammer of a .38 being cocked behind him. The same kind of gun he knew Carmine Rizzo used.

"You're goddamned right it's gonna get ugly," Carmine said. "Starting with you."

"What the hell are you doing?" Mimi shrieked from the couch. "Put that damned thing away before he takes it from you."

Quinn turned just enough to let Carmine see his grin. "Listen to the lady, stupid. You're not going to use it anyhow."

"No kidding?" Carmine said. "What makes you so goddamned sure?"

"Because shooting me is going to make your life more complicated than it already is. Especially when you have to explain to Rothmann why you shot me. And what you were doing here in the first place."

"Bullshit. Rothmann knows I'm here."

"Bullshit," Quinn repeated. "Rothmann would never let you muscle in on one of Archie's gambling dens. He knows better than to risk a war over a hellhole like this. But you?" He laughed. "You're just greedy enough to think you could get away with it. Dumb enough, too."

Carmine didn't laugh. "For a washed-up pug, you've got some imagination."

"Nah, just a good pair of eyes." He motioned to the unconscious Van Dorn punk on the floor. "You brought those two fat cats in the tuxes here tonight, didn't you? Sold them on a can't-miss way to buy themselves a piece of the action. For just a grand or so apiece, they'd get a cut of this place, plus the satisfaction of screwing over Archie Doyle in the process. Any smart guy would've laughed in your face, but a couple of well-heeled dopes like them, well…"

Mimi dropped her glass of champagne. "Jesus Christ, Carmine! How the hell does he know all that?"

"Relax," Carmine said. "He's just guessing. He doesn't know shit."

"Sure I do." Quinn looked at Mimi. "People like to talk. And Archie likes to listen."

Mimi's eyes went wide. "I…it wasn't me, Terry. I swear." She pointed back to Carmine. "It was him! He cooked the whole thing up. Him and that lousy bastard Joey. They lied to me. They…"

Carmine came around Quinn to get a clear shot at Madeline. Quinn yanked Carmine's gun arm up and hit him with two short rights to the jaw.

Carmine went limp, held up by Quinn holding his left wrist. He took the gun out of his hand and let Carmine drop to the floor.

He opened the cylinder and pocketed the bullets. He tossed the empty .38 on the couch next to Mimi.

She flinched when the gun hit the cushion. She dropped her head into her hands and wept. "Jesus Christ, Terry. Jesus Christ, what am I gonna do now? Don't kill me. Please don't…"

"Knock it off. Just tell me where's the money you owe Archie?"

"It's gone," she wailed. "We had a couple of great weeks that put us way ahead, so Joey started skimming a little from the extra we earned."

"Gambling?" Quinn asked.

Madeline nodded. "He found himself into Carmine pretty deep. Soon, the extra we were earning wasn't enough to cover what we owed, so we cut into the rest of the take. He figured Archie would never miss it."

"Guess what?" Quinn said. "He did."

"Carmine told him he'd forgive the debt if he could help us swindle these two rich boys out of a couple of grand. Make them think they were buying a piece of this place."

"Where's the money they brought with them?"

Mimi lifted her face from her hands. Her mascara smeared all over her face. "Terry, please. I…"

He kicked the table over. Champagne bottle and glasses flew. "The Van Dorn money, Mimi. Now!"

Slowly, she pulled the briefcase out from under the couch and she set it on her lap. She fumbled with the locks, but got them open. It looked to be about two grand in greenbacks. Just like he'd been told. Enough for the rich kids to buy a piece of the place.

Or at least think they had.

He wondered how long it would've been before they got killed in a convenient mugging once they realized Carmine and Joey had fooled them.

Mimi grinned up at him and ran her tongue along the edges of her teeth. "It's all right here, sugar. Two grand in cold cash. Enough to pay back Archie what we owe him."

She lowered the lid of the briefcase enough for him to look down her dress. Her smeared mascara gave her a mean, desperate look. "Enough for you and me to blow town and have ourselves some *real* fun somewhere. What do you say?"

Quinn shut the case and yanked it off her lap. The Van Dorn kid groaned as he began to stir on the floor.

"I'd say you're going to have a couple of angry playmates when they wake up in a few minutes."

Mimi sat back on the couch and folded her arms across her chest. Modesty had returned. "What am I supposed to tell them when they do?"

"That the deal is off and you'll pay them back with your own money. Tell them this is still Doyle's place and if they don't like it, they'll have to answer to Archie. And me."

"That's swell," Mimi said. "Just swell. But who's gonna tell Joey? Somebody's gonna have to tell that crazy son of a bitch what happened and it sure as hell ain't gonna be me. He'll beat the hell outta me for this."

He locked the briefcase. "No he won't."

"Yeah?" Mimi said. "How do you know?"

He smiled as he opened the door. "Trust me."

*****

He shut the door behind him as he went out through the crowd of gamblers. If any of them had heard the commotion in the office, none of them let on. They were too busy poring over the tables, looking for a way to chisel in on the action.

The blonde boy in the tuxedo was nowhere in sight. Probably back with Mummy and Daddy up on Fifth Avenue or wherever that type holed up.

He wondered if the stupid bastard would ever realize that Quinn had actually saved his life.

Otis was back at his piano, pawing out an old Jolson number on the ivories. Quinn made sure he saw him drop another twenty in his tip jar. He patted the piano as he passed by. "Safe and sound, Otis. I'm a man of my word."

"Night's still young," Otis called after him.

*****

Issue 1

Quinn's fatigue returned as he walked to an all-night drugstore right around the corner and called Archie from the payphone in the back.

Archie came on the line quick, "How'd it go, kid?"

"I got the cash the swells were going to kick in for a share of the place. Two grand, just like Joey told us."

"Good. Any bloodshed?"

"Not much, boss. You told me to go easy, so I did."

Doyle didn't sound convinced. "Terry…"

"I had to knock the Van Dorn brat around and I stopped Carmine from shooting Mimi. They're banged up but alive, I promise."

"What about that bastard Rizzo," Doyle said. "Where'd you park his Plymouth?"

"Right across the street from the place, just like you wanted. I made sure I left the keys in the car for the cops to find."

"Good. I'll call our friend and tip him off about Joey's body being in Carmine's trunk." Quinn knew their friend was Andrew Carmichael, Commissioner of the New York Police Department. "If they get there fast enough, maybe they'll nab Carmine in Mimi's place. The Van Dorn punk too. Give them back-stabbing bastards somethin' to chew on."

Quinn hadn't slept in two whole nights and was too tired to care anymore. He had Archie's money and that's what mattered. "You know best, boss."

"Goddamned right, kid," Archie laughed. "Goddamned right. Now get some sleep. You earned it."

Quinn hung up the phone and let Archie make his calls. He squeezed out of the phone booth and ordered a coffee from the counterman. It was late-night coffee—lukewarm and bitter—but it was better than no coffee at all. It had enough of a kick to keep him from falling asleep in the cab on the way home.

He played the whole thing out in his mind while he sipped his coffee. He had to hand it to Archie. They didn't call him The Duke for nothing; he always knew just what to do. Once he found out about the skim, he had Quinn pick up Joey and lean on him until he cracked.

He'd thought Joey dying like that had complicated things, but not Archie. Once Joey spilled about the scheme to team up with Carmine Rizzo, Archie figured out a way to put Joey to work for him one last time. He'd prove more useful in death than he'd ever been in life.

He'd ordered someone to steal Carmine's car from in front of Lady M's dive and brought to him. Then he stuck Joe's body in the trunk and drove the Plymouth back to where he'd found it—right in front of Lady M's.

The result? Joey was dead. Carmine was going to jail for his murder and Mimi was put on notice. And Doyle gets his money back. Hell, Doyle had even gotten Howard Rothmann to sign off on the whole thing. Why not? It gave Chief Carmichael a chance to show the city he was a crime fighter after all. Score one for the good guys.

But Quinn had learned long ago that there were no good guys and bad guys in The Life. Just guys out to make a buck and guys who died trying.

Guys like Archie Doyle and men like Terry Quinn who worked for them.

He drained his coffee and paid his tab. He'd just gotten outside the coffee shop when he heard the sirens of the squad cars racing along 14th Street. He walked to the corner and saw the cops had already opened the trunk of Carmine Rizzo's Plymouth. He saw Joey's body was inside, just like Quinn had left it.

He watched another group of cops drag Mimi and Carmine into the street in handcuffs. The Van Dorn brat wobbled out last.

Mimi was wailing, this time for real. It took three cops to push Carmine into the back of the squad car. The Van Dorn punk just looked woozy and ridiculous. Handcuffs and tuxes went together just about as well as cops and dead men in trunks.

Issue 1

A couple of uniforms recognized Quinn and waved. Why not? He was on Doyle's payroll, too. Just a friend, standing on the corner in the middle of the night. With a suitcase in his hand.

Quinn smiled and waved back. Then hailed a cab going the other way.

Spill Site

by Matthew C. Funk

Big Dan got the bad news from Eric Delacey, his Service Manager, just as a knock hammered his front door. He lowered the cell—Delacey still booming on about the spill site—and shot a look across his living room. Rain hit hard enough to almost dent the windows. He hoped it would wash away whoever was knocking.

"So how bad is bad, Eric?"

"About as bad as it gets. Storm's taken the waste right over our levees. Twenty years of dumping is pouring right for the lot."

'For the lot' meant for Big Dan's house, right next door. He blew air through his broke-veined nose to clear the pinch in his chest. It didn't help. Neither did the knocking.

Big Dan considered switching his den light off. The knocker might get the message.

"EPA going to get involved in this?"

"You kidding me? We'll be lucky if the showroom isn't a swimming pool of ethylene glycol and sulfuric acid."

Turning off the lamp turned the knocking into a slamming.

"So how do we contain this, Eric?"

Issue 1

Silence. For the hundredth time this year, Big Dan wondered why he bothered paying apes like Delacey. If he could run the Chevy dealership himself, they'd all be out on their dumb asses.

"Call me back when you have a fucking answer." Big Dan hung up. He lumbered to the door, worked both deadbolts and yanked open the oversized knob.

The roar of the storm barged in, bringing water by the bucket to spatter his slippers. It hazed the figure into a ghost. For a moment, Big Dan could have sworn he was looking at his daughter, Andrea, from decades back.

But Andrea knew better than to visit.

"Who're you?" His tone left no question that the answer would only piss him off more.

"Papa," the girl said, forcing a smile while the rest of her shivered in a soaked-through hoodie, water pouring up from inside her Vans. "It's Darlene."

"Darly?" Big Dan was surprised to feel the brick in his chest soften. The sensation was like a wish he'd long forgotten being answered. He nearly smiled. "What the hell are you doing out in this weather?"

"I'm on my own now," she said, tucking hands embedded in her sweatshirt pockets tighter about her middle. "Mama and I had a parting of the ways."

Big Dan grunted. The kid was probably looking for charity, ducking out on her welfare mother for a taste of her grandpa the dealership owner's wealth.

Still, Darly could be a welcome distraction. Ten years parted left a lot of catching up to do. Besides, anything that would rile Andrea suited him fine.

"Come on in, then," Big Dan said, waving her on. He considered wrapping an arm around her willow-branch body, something to soothe that shivering, but thought better. It would only soak them both. "Kick your shoes off, though."

She did. Big Dan scowled to see a dark rainbow of chemicals fringing their soles. The rogue's gallery of toxic waste Delacey had listed echoed: Carburetor cleaner, transmission fluid, battery acid, antifreeze, oil.

All headed out of the Mississippi mire to swamp his business. His house. Him.

Big Dan gave a wistful look across the street to where the dealership sign should have glowed. The storm had stolen the power, but he imagined it, lit and looming bigger than one of those faggy euro coupes. Potter Chevrolet of Wiggins—a declaration of dominance over his plot of land.

He slammed the door rather than look at the flood swallowing that land a moment longer.

Darly was pivoting, taking in Big Dan's den with baby-doll eyes wide under the seaweed fringe of her black-dyed hair. He ate up her awe—her wonder at the garfish with its prehistoric snarl jutting over the mantle, the out-sized furniture of imported leather and antique wood, the clusters of photos, fleur-de-lis and American flags.

He'd enjoy his castle as long as he could. To hell with the doubters—his dead wife, his pastor, the Sheriff. It was fucking great to be the king.

"So, Darly," he said, clasping her shoulder and steering her shocked face around for his stare to savor. "Tell me how your bitch of a mother is."

*****

The photo albums were all organized, but Big Dan yanked them from the cupboards and stacked them on his teak coffee table. They tiered in towers, forty years of family memories and booming business. It reminded him of the Norman fortresses he used to model out of hub cabs behind his old man's scrapyard.

"We don't really have to do this, Papa," Darly said, "if you need to sleep, I mean."

He turned to her and sipped Dewar's through his smile. It felt odd to smile without bitterness on the backs of his teeth. The whole sensation—genuine happiness—felt odd, a warm softness running from his neck to his bulging belly, like the filling of a birthday cake.

"I'm a night owl and an early bird both, Darly, don't you worry." He put a canny bend in his grin. The girl mirrored it. Big Dan figured this apple fell right onto the roots of the tree.

"Okay, then." She perked her plucked eyebrows. "Think I could have a scotch, though?"

He chuckled in time with a wagging finger. The girl had his guts, too.

Her hair was dark, but Big Dan bet there'd be his rye-colored roots under the dye. Her jaw was slender, but her chin had the same die-cut square. Her sharp eyes, her hard brow, her high cheeks—all pieces of his mirror turned into something beautiful.

"You'll settle with that coffee, kiddo."

Darly shrugged and rubbed her arm. She'd insisted on keeping the hoodie on. Big Dan insisted she at least change into dry jeans, for the sake of his couch if nothing else. He wondered if she'd kept her damp panties on or went bare.

Was that wrong to wonder about his granddaughter? Big Dan smirked to himself as he sorted out an album. As if he gave a tin shit about "wrong."

"Here we go," he said, raising up from popping knees and ambling over to Darly with the album. "2002. Your last visit, right?"

"I was six, so, yeah, I guess so." She fixed a hopeful look on him. "Is Grandma in this one?"

He nodded. They paged through it. Image after image of his wife, his pairs of sons and daughters, his four grandkids. They huddled together on picnic tables at the park ground on the 4th of July, stood before the Christmas tree's glister, crammed around the Thanksgiving spread. Every picture gleamed with tight smiles and flashbulb happiness.

Dan didn't look at the smiles. He studied the eyes. He wanted to run his fingertip over their hard pebbles; rub them like Braille to feel if a hidden story could be read.

"Everybody looks so happy," Darly said, sober and slouched. "When did things go bad?"

"When they grew up and quit listening," Big Dan said. He flipped pages faster. "And when your grandmother died."

The truth was that things were always kind of bad. Big Dan and his wife, Allie, had tried to set the kids right. He'd spared no expense and no punishment.

The slightest show of weakness in these kids—bad grades, poor performance on the field, teenage romance—and he'd get the whole family to make fun of them. The tape recorders in their bedrooms and the late-night spying discovered their secrets and gave him grounds to correct them with beatings. And every time he got back talk, he'd lock them in the basement. Hell, he'd forgotten Andrea down there for a day and a half one time.

All that discipline, and still they'd broken bad. Turned sneaky. Gone bitter. Given up.

Big Dan shut the album and grabbed another at random off the stack. He flipped through, not exchanging a word with Darly.

"Everything looks so pretty," Darly said, hands clasped in her jacket pockets again. "Guess that's what money gets you: A lot of pretty."

That's all she said. And that was fine by Big Dan. It was enough to know she understood—knew what was necessary in life and what his family had given up.

Andrea gave up on everything but an endless course of scumbag baby daddies. Chrissie, she was a sour old maid at 35 with love only for cats and self-cutting. Dan Junior and Dick, they were in and out of the pen, the church and the poorhouse.

How he'd fought for those kids. Fought without compromise or remorse.

All they did was fight back.

He slapped the album closed midway and tossed it back on the table. A belt of scotch only made the cramped burn in him worse.

All that fighting, and now the only thing he had left— his Chevy store, his sign and his castle by the lake—would be lost to him.

The storm slammed the windows like the laughter of the mob. The chemicals had slipped their stink through his window seals. The burn in him just sank deeper no matter how long he drank.

Darly lifted it with a touch of his hand.

He set down the glass and found her eyes waiting. They were carved wise like his, but wanton. Interest glowed through their weary cores.

"Can we look at another?"

"I got a better idea," Big Dan said, before he even really knew what it was.

"What's that?"

"Let's get out of here."

"Where?" The eagerness snuck into her lips and stretched them wide.

"New Orleans."

"Really?" She giggled. Big Dan felt like giggling too. He couldn't even remember the last time he'd felt like that. Probably some time before his old man began to use the buckle of the belt to whip him with, and that was his first memory—stretched onto the stove, his nose against burner soot, as the iron gouged his bare ass.

"Yeah, let's get out there and settle in."

"But this place is so nice."

Big Dan waved that away. "We'll find another nice place. This place is done for."

She didn't take a moment to think—just nodded. Enthusiasm lunged Big Dan to his feet without even feeling his knees ache. He didn't leave Darly's eyes.

There was hope and youth enough there for the both of them—the bright breed of youth that still believed in flight and fresh starts.

"I'll pack my things," he said, tipping her chin with a finger. She lifted her grin, crooked little teeth showing. "You get drinks and snacks for the road."

He wouldn't bring much. Enough to live on until New Orleans.

Living was what this was about—getting out from the toxic flood, the tonnage of the business, the wreck of his family.

Darly skipped to the kitchen as if the pounding of the storm were less than just a nightmare.

*****

Big Dan studied his razor before tossing it into the sink.

He'd give up shaving awhile. Go bearded on a fishing boat, reeling in catfish and gar and perch with Darly reading a romance novel by the beer cooler.

Besides, it was his old man's razor.

He'd bring the toothpaste but leave the cologne. Bring the dog tags but leave the cufflinks. Bring the watch he'd bought with his first paycheck but ditch the engagement bracelet from Allie.

He dropped Allie's perfume into his Dopp kit for Darly, though.

She reminded him more of his late wife with every heartbeat: Her spirit, her wit, her girlish manner. Allie had been two years younger than Darly when they married, but the teen had a bounce to her that the burden of growing up under Andrea's tyranny hadn't crushed. It had only gone clever.

Big Dan appreciated that cleverness as he looked himself over in the mirror, popping the collar of his Polo shirt. He was plenty clever, too. Always had been. Having to get around his fucker of a father gave him the smarts and drive to seize what he wanted no matter what.

He left the dealership keys on his bedside table. Potter Chevy had been won hard: Cutthroat deals. Backstabbing marketing. Backroom nights passing cash into the hands of the fat bastards on the zoning boards, the town council and the inspection office.

It was all worthless now. The flood of the spill sites saw to that.

Time to liquidate.

He crammed the Dopp into a satchel bloated with his safe's six-figure cash supply, slid into his work boots and turned out the light on ten pairs of Italian loafers.

It made him want to whistle Dixie as he sauntered for the kitchen to meet Darly.

He spotted Chrissie instead.

Big Dan frowned. It was impossible not to when one saw Chrissie—the woman's worry lines had taken a washboard to her face. Anything that might've been pretty about her was sagged like a saddlebag.

Her scowl was turned to Darly. She gave her dad a flick of her eyes. They were fixed on the .357 in Darly's hand.

"Chris?" Big Dan said. The frosting feeling in his chest soured and sank heavy. It made him aware of the air choked by stinging chemical from the spill. "What's going on?"

Darly swung the gun at him. Something struggled unsaid behind the stitch of her lips. The affectionate interest in her eyes was now a desperate hunger.

"She shot Andrea is what's going on," Chrissie said, a lifetime of Benson & Hedges croaking her tone. "Shot her own mother. Put her in a coma."

"Shut up," Darly said, snapping the Magnum back at Chrissie.

"Might've killed her. Might've killed her own mother."

"Shut up!"

"Darly," Big Dan began. The gun's aim cut him off, almost swayed him. His body felt like brick, head like a balloon, chest burning.

"I came here to tell you because you must've changed your damn phone number on us again," Chrissie said. Big Dan ignored her. He cared only for his granddaughter, beautiful and rabid, and for getting out with her.

"Darly, we can still work this out," he said, forcing his legs forward. They managed one step. It made the women flinch.

"How? Lawyers?" Darly smiled, all sweet poison. "You'd lose."

"We can just get out of here," Big Dan said, demanding another step but failing.

"Are you serious?" Chrissie yelled. "She shot Andrea, Pa! She's going to prison!"

"I'd take care of you," Big Dan said.

Darly's stare softened. He stepped toward it.

Softness only survived a moment. The blaze came back to her eyes, hotter than before, with pain fueling it.

"I've heard that before," Darly said, smile twitching as something in her fractured, "from my bitch of a mother."

Big Dan reached. Darly's gun boomed.

He came to after a long instant like snipped film. His cheek was on the Milanese tile. His body felt like someone else's.

The stink of cordite, car fluid, and the sweet penny smell of blood stained everything he breathed.

Chrissie lay a few feet away, eyes gaping like the fist-sized hole in her throat. He could hear the front door open. The storm howled in Darly's exit.

Big Dan gathered his breaths. Each had to be wrestled in. Each brought more strength. He collected enough to try taking his feet.

It took half a minute—shoving his palms into the blood gumming the floor, bending his knees, head screaming like it had when his Pa lashed him.

He fell.

He breathed deep twice.

He fought up again.

Big Dan's house wheeled around him as he went upright and staggered for the door. He let it spin. He let his nerves scream and collapse. He had to get to Darly.

She was escape. Life. Salvation for them both.

The rain embraced him with a beating: Punched his head. Pushed his shoulders. Yelled into the pits of his ears.

He wouldn't let his old man beat him this time—the girl was still in sight.

Darly jogged ahead through toxic mire that gripped over her ankles. She'd made it to Chrissie's Toyota truck parked under the Potter Chevy sign. Big Dan failed to call out, lungs filled with caulk.

She fumbled at the lock.

He forced shuffle after shuffle through the sludge, until his boot hit highway tarmac.

She wrenched the door open.

He drove himself faster.

She was haloed by the interior light, face bright as a baby photo, eyes just like his.

He fought words out.

"Darly! Take me with you!"

The fight robbed his wind. His next step faltered. His knees broke the flood mire, buckled on the highway, pitched him forward.

Darly looked back in time to watch Big Dan fall.

He watched, face half in the muck, as she slid into the Toyota without pausing and started it up.

He tried to watch her drive away. Tried harder than he ever had at anything. Needed to see if she at least looked back.

The flood rose to shut his open eyes.

A Clean White Sun

by Mike Wilkerson

Waiting for her.

Hours spent kneeling and praying with her paperback copy of Falconer in my hands, the book's cover speckled black with her blood. The terrazzo floor is cold and hard beneath knees raw and burning. Unrelenting, I rest my head on the edge of the bed's bare mattress, close my eyes and wait for her.

Fading. Booze and Morpheus proceed to conspire against me, allowing only micro-second cuts, flashbacks of a final blinding glance. Numbers blip on a gas pump as Audrey smiles at me through the passenger side window, holding the book she's been reading to her chest, the white sun on her mahogany skin. I can smell the sweetness of her perfume cutting through the thick vapor of oil and gas and stink of this world.

Eyes flickering. Images floating.

The world's gone red and I'm reaching, grabbing for her. She's only a few steps away but like lost halcyon days, never within my grasp.

Spinning free.

*****

St. Petersburg, Florida—Tuesday, July 10th, 1979

Issue 1

The phone ringing and cutting cathartic tendencies short. I grab the receiver and check the time on a glowing bedside clock—11:00—straight up.

"Yeah."

"Preston Street. Head south off 15th Avenue, a few houses up on your left. Little white shack, bare yard, maroon Crown Vic in the drive. You'll know it when you see it. Back door opens into the kitchen."

Standing and straightening out stiffened knees. Tender skin breaks open and blood trickles down my shins and seeps through brown gabardine pants. The pain feels good.

"How many?"

Freddy sniffs. "Two Bloods and a skinny-ass whitebread. Cats be strapped and straight up flyin'. Bad scene, my brotha."

"Whitebread—the cousin?"

A grunt. "Dig it. Half-assed prison tats on both forearms. Lightning bolts and I do mean *Shazam!* mothafucka."

"My nigga."

Freddy sneezes. "Just remember that, cuz."

My pulse spikes as the connection buzzes a flatline. I drop the phone, slip on my shoes and grab a black, sweat-streaked t-shirt from a month-old pile of dirty clothes. I don't even notice the sour aroma of body odor anymore.

Two clean throwdown pieces sit next to a battered gold shield on my dining room table. I clip the shield to my belt and then remember where I'm going, what I'm preparing to do and the price I'm willing to pay.

What I've already paid.

Past and present collide and my head does a drunken dizzy dance. I throw the television through the living room wall. Picture tubes explode. Chunks of plaster scatter across the floor and dust fills the air. I toss my shield into the wreckage and grab the hardware, goose a line of flake off the kitchen counter and make my way out the door.

Rolling. Constricted capillaries distend to make room for the river of blood gushing through my veins. Scenarios circulating. She's been missing going on three days straight, her country bumpkin jailbird cousin off the grid just as long—and alive or dead, she's already a statistic.

Childhood gone.

Innocence gone.

Morning headlines:

POOR JENNY HUGHES, TWELVE YEARS OLD AND JUST PLAIN GONE.

I grab another gear, drop the pedal, kill the yellow light at 34th Street.

Running east on 15th Avenue South. Hot. This city at night is a sweat lodge and visions appear in the darkness which I know aren't there—hope in the faces of the hard young brothers who sit on front porch stoops of cribs gone to wrack and ruin. They're guzzling malt liquor out of bumpers wrapped in brown paper bags. They're smoking Kool Milds. They're yapping about poontang. They see me with anxious eyes but don't care unless I'm buying. The dollar rules, along with despair and destitution.

Teeth gnashing. Perspiration flows down my back and I'm sweat-stuck to the seat as I ease my foot down on the gas, the rumbling of the 'Cuda's Hemi losing the battle against fleeting minutes screaming *Tick!—Tick!—Tick!* in my ears even as a realization begins pounding in my skull:

I didn't call in backup because I've got no one left.

I've burned all the bridges.

Chances taken will belong only to me.

*****

Issue 1

Regret drives me. I'd given up being a husband to Audrey a year earlier. The detective shield changed everything. Days, weeks at a time away from her, 1976 as a stone blur. Faces—dead faces and scared faces and blank faces crippled me. Shakedowns and kickbacks were justified in my mind to ease the pain, making myself believe I was right.

I ran the gamut even as the grind wore me down. I didn't sleep. I didn't eat. But against my will, she held me together.

She held me together until she fell apart.

*****

Childhood stomping grounds revisited.

Preston Street. Beneath the untrimmed Sabal Palmetto trees and shabby live oaks, faded turquoise and peach-colored houses loiter on barren sandy yards. Rusty bicycles with flat tires and busted chains. Old pots and pans filled with typhoid-infested water being lapped up by oversized mutts on log chains. Trash strewn from here to fucking there.

I cruise by my destination at an idle, a tiny clapboard bungalow with peeling white paint and aluminum foil taped to the windows, a shroud for keeping the heat out or the glare of violence in. I don't stare and I don't slow down. I scope the scene—this burg is disco dead. Check it—I'm just another Southside nigger out for a late-night joyride.

One block down, I park in front of a vacant lot void of spillover light from street lamps and kill the engine. One more hit and the blow clears my head, amplifies minutes giving way to seconds yelling *TICK!—TICK!—TICK!* while sweat runs down my nose and onto the hardware as I re-check their loads by feel in the darkness.

Ready—the .45 in my hand, the .357 backup strapped to my ankle. Jaw clamped shut, teeth ready to crack and implications leapfrogging in my head as I open the car door, knowing I've got this one last chance to stop, call it in and do this on the level.

My feet hit the ground and I'm running across the street, sprinting and tripping my way through a backyard overgrown with crabgrass clumps and scruffy orange trees. Limbs slap my face, scrape my arms. The gun is light in my hand and those scenarios and implications are winding on a closed circuit.

Knowing.

I've got one last chance to make this right.

*****

Friday, May 1st, 1977. A seven-hour trip would put us in Atlanta, Georgia, Audrey's hometown. Friends. Family. Home-cooked meals. I got off early on a Wednesday and we would leave that same day.

Audrey met me at the front door, almond-shaped eyes like green pools of water and a smile on her face, the first one I'd noticed in months.

Me, making up lost time: We made love before leaving and she cried in my arms.

Me, making up lies: "Things will change, baby. I promise."

*****

Humping it over chain-link fences, my heart working like a piston in a top fuel sled. Trash cans bang together as feral cats squeal and dance across their metal lids. A backyard dog goes stone batshit.

A kid's voice from somewhere behind me says, "Who dat?"

A mother responds: "You's don't be worrying about who's out there. You's just get yo black ass inside and shut dat window!"

One more backyard, one more fence and I've reached the bungalow, sucking air while staring at a back door painted red. I feel like a sinner entering hell for the first and last time.

I steady my breathing and ask God if He's listening.

He doesn't answer.

I take the silence as approval and kick the door off its fucking hinges.

*****

I was inside paying for gas and buying Audrey a Dr. Pepper when I heard the spattering of shots fired. AK-47 on full auto. I sprinted outside. A blue Chevy Impala with dirt-covered plates laid rubber out into 34th Street traffic. People scrambling and screaming, horns blowing.

Dead in my tracks.

Her blood sprayed onto the passenger side window.

On my knees in a lake of shattered glass, holding her in my arms.

Her blood sprayed everywhere.

*****

Sightline. On a gold velour couch sits a fat-ass Blood with a lopsided fro and wearing a red shirt the size of a tent. He's eating ice cream from the container. Next to him sprawls a rail-thin and shirtless white boy with blue tattoos on his forearms. Lightning bolts. They're hittin'. They're buzzin'. The glass-topped coffee table in front of them is stacked with dope and guns. The air inside smells stale, dead.

Chaos as I cross the kitchen into the front room. Music blaring and lava lamps burning low buffer the two stunned faces with glassy jaundiced eyes. Tunnel vision as the .45 spits—two in the face, and the juiced-up cracker's shaved head snaps back, a bloody halo spattering on the white wall behind him like a repulsive modern art masterpiece. I want to linger. I want to ask him why.

Ears ringing as I take another step.

Fat Albert's stuck in the couch, trembling and struggling to get on his feet. Garbled sounds are coming from his mouth. He takes two in the chest with a jerk. He coughs up a glob of blood into his ice cream before falling sideways into his partner's lap with a confused and questioning look on his bulging face.

Head spinning, blood pounding.

Thinking is a liability. I forego the temptation as I haul ass through an open bedroom door to my left, .45 leveled in front of me and jumping headlong into the kind of nightmare I foolishly believed could exist only for me.

I don't want to see her like this.

I don't want to see Jenny Hughes laid bare and tied to the bed with the soiled white sheets turned cherry beneath her. I don't want to see her soaking wet hair, dark and stringy while sticking to her face and mouth. I don't want to see the yellowing bruises on the soft alabaster skin of her thrashing arms and legs.

I only want to fall away; for a minute, a day.

A goddamn lifetime.

Strobes of light begin pulsating in my head and the dizziness is back along with a nauseous clarity. The bright-as-day room. The bed. The cheap, walnut-veneered chest of drawers with the busted mirror shoved against a jizz-stained eggshell-white wall. The girl and the empty bottles of codeine-laden cough syrup they've forced down her throat.

Me.

Everyone and everything is in their place, but only the sight of him has stopped my world from spinning out of control on its greased-up axis.

And he's straight zoned.

Big Stud Blood's in his birthday suit, holding a twelve-gauge pump and fumbling with fat red shells. His feet are moving like he's standing on burning hot coals and he's not even paying attention to what's in front of him—

because with his posse out front no one should've ever made it this far.

His eyes find me, blink once, twice and then go "OH MY GOD!" wide.

*****

I knew the reasons why, knew the potential implications. The kickbacks. The shakedowns. The time away from Audrey spent living another life, making the excuse that I was owed the money I took. Like a rodent, I'd taken the cheddar from their hands and then tried to turn full circle on the very men who paid me to keep my mouth shut. I was naïve. I thought I could walk away from the game without consequence.

I thought the badge meant I was untouchable.

*****

Scared—another strange face and the girl is screaming bloody fucking murder. I put one in Stud's thigh. He drops. He cries. Arterial damage and a bloody geyser erupts.

Move—

My pocketknife slices through the ropes. She rolls up in a ball, covering herself down there. My hand on her shoulder and Jenny balls up tighter. She's so small.

Move—

The brother on the floor yells. I wipe and toss the .45, retrieve the .357 from my ankle and put one in his gut. Lungs push rotten air out through his mouth and into my face. I gag. I aim for his nappy head. The girl whimpers and I see Jenny Hughes's future as a funneling black whirlpool and my mind screams: *Let him fucking bleed!*

I don't take the next shot.

I'll let him fucking bleed.

Move—

I clean and drop the .357. I wrap the girl in blood-stained sheets, throw her over my shoulder and head straight for the front door, slipping and sliding while making tracks through the puddle of human fluids and melted ice cream before being thrust out into the sultry night.

Booking for my car straight down the middle of Preston Street, the 'Cuda sitting a million miles away. Lungs burning. Legs giving out. Neighborhood porch lights click on and hidden faces appear in doorways, but nobody says a threatening word and no one tries to stop me.

Running on fumes and I'm a million fucking miles away.

I'm at the passenger side door, a stitch like a blade in my side. I stash Jenny, start my ride and stomp the gas. Tires burn, smoke and then grab hold of the pavement. The steering wheel goes loose in my hand as the front end kisses the ground goodbye and I'm flying.

Hemi stroking—end of the block and I hit the corner in fourth gear, speedometer knocking on 60, an orange-red blur slicing through the night. I don't bother looking back.

The hopeless will continue buying and selling in the streets.

The scared will continue standing still for fear of deadly retribution.

*****

Off duty night moves. For the next two years after the day they took Audrey away from me, I burned this town to the ground. I took weeks of stored-up vacation time off and dug for names, promising anyone who stood in my way that hell would be a better choice than me in front of them, me behind them.

I got names. I got places. I formed big bad habits.

Issue 1

Supplication. I began praying with her book in my hands, the last thing Audrey would ever touch, begging for the reprieve I would never get.

*****

Heading north on 16th Street South. Traffic's late-night thin. I drop my speed down to the limit. Eyes ahead. Eyes to the rearview. A cruiser passes me going the opposite direction, the uniform's eyes strafing my ride. Dicey. Window rolled halfway down, a blood-spattered nigger driving a boss crate with a brutally traumatized white girl in tow. No questions would be asked.

Goosebumps. The sticky warm night feels cold and I roll the window up. Jenny's hunched down in the passenger seat, her moaning like a constant electric hum. Primal—she's shutting the world out.

I put a hand on her arm. She flinches. She kicks and bites and claws my hand bloody. I reach across the seat and pull her close, her thin body going limp as the sobbing of incoherent words are being choked and jerked from her mouth.

My voice is placid, telling her the same untruths I told Audrey, over and over and over:

"Everything will be okay, sugar. I promise."

*****

There were two of them. Two second-tier crackers I'd sent to Union County for a deuce. Time served. Shyster's working overtime.

They served six months.

I took six months from them and they ripped my fucking life apart.

I won't make excuses to justify. I opened their stomachs while they were still alive and watched them die a slow and bloody death in an abandoned Midtown warehouse for two long days. I'd do it again. Even after the swarming greenbottle flies and the smell of men losing

control and their begging, I'd do it again. I've already crossed the line
and I'll keep crossing it until He hears me.
   Until He understands what living is doing to me.

*****

Next morning, early.

I throw my shield on my Sergeant Brice's desk. He's
sitting in his shirtsleeves with blue veins plumped out on
his forearms and biceps, a reluctant seat shiner. He looks
at the shield, lights a cigarette and then stares me down
while talking in his raspy phlegmatic voice.

"Don't let 'em beat you like this, Mike. Don't let
this...society we live in and what happened to Audrey
dictate your life." He points at me with the cigarette
crushed between two nicotine-stained fingers. "We've
been through this a dozen times in the last two years, so
just pick up your badge and walk the fuck back out that
door."

Society. Ghosts. One and the same.

In a nigger drawl, I give him a bullshit self-serving
excuse. "Yeah, wouldn't want the department to lose
another token jig." Bulge those eyes. Shuffle those feet.
"What would da colored folk think then?" I shake my
head, dig down deep for a grin, come up snake eyes.
"Listen...it's time, Sarge. We've both known it for a while
now. I'm no good for this anymore. I just can't fucking do
it."

Brice stabs out his cigarette in a heavy glass ashtray
filled with two days worth of half-smoked butts. He
doesn't blink, doesn't raise his voice. "Token—don't lay
that crap on me. I've never been that person, Mike. If you
want to call it quits, fine. If you want to make excuses,
fine." The corner of his mouth jerks up and he leans
forward on his desk, lacing his battle-scarred hands
together. "But you're not being rational. And you're a
mess, kid. I can smell you from here."

Issue 1

I want to respond, but have nothing left to say. Sarge still has plenty, though. He takes a breath and lets fly.

"Don't know if you heard, but the Hughes girl showed up last night." A head shake. "Bad shape."

Calm and easy. "Yeah?"

His steel-gray eyes run down and then up my body before settling back on my face. "Somebody dropped her off downtown at the hospital ER and split. Left a note with her. Just a scribbled address, but it was the right address. Fucking bloodbath. Her white trash loser cousin and a couple other model citizens. Looks like the cousin was selling her for cash and dope to his buddies. Him and a fat boy were DOA. The third guy managed to crawl outside, but bled out on the back porch steps. Femoral artery and gut shot. That's a hard way to eat it."

I shrug. "Doesn't sound like much of a loss."

"Neighbors must feel the same way." Brice snatches up a pen and gives a rat-a-tat-tat on the desk. "At least six shots were fired but nobody heard anything. And not one person got a plate number or even noticed the make of the getaway car. Tire-burn marks for twenty feet and no one saw a goddamn thing. Sled had to be a beast to lay rubber like that."

Blood thumping. Mouth like cotton. I dry gulp and nix the car conversation: "Say what? Telling me no one at the ER had anything worth a damn to add? Not one motherfucking thing?" I shake my head, lay it on thick. "Seems kinda hard to believe, I mean, joint's jumpin' all day every day. Shiiiit—cops and staff must've been all over that motherfucking place!"

"You'd think. But all they heard was the admittance door buzzer. Girl was sitting outside in front of the door. She was sitting there alone in her own fucking blood and just...humming to herself. One of the attendants lost his chow and set off a chain reaction. Whoever dropped the girl off slipped in and out *tout suite*."

I lick my lips. "How is the—?"

Brice cuts me off. "I think you know how she is, Mike."

My right foot starts tapping out of control. My brain's telling my foot to play it cool. Play it Billy D. Fucking Williams cool. I spread my legs, dig my toes into the carpet and lock my knees. I don't answer him.

Brice, chewing his lower lip bloody. "Come on, you've seen this kind of thing before. Jesus. You know how she is today and you know how she'll be twenty goddamn years from now."

I don't push him. I put my shades on beneath the buzzing and flickering fluorescent lights. "Yeah, I know, Sarge. I'll see ya around, huh?"

Eyes down, Brice bobs his head of thick black hair, palms flat on the desk. "Yeah."

Through the cubicles, through the rows of questioning eyes watching me. My legs nearly give way as I step from the building's sterile air conditioning out into the heat of a new day. I breathe deep—dig that nasty smell oozing from my pores, snuffing out the fresh summer jasmine.

I walk through the parking lot and to my car, the blood-smeared seats covered with beach towels and already frying pan hot. My stomach gurgles. I open the door and heave up yellow bile. I put my head between my knees and mutter the one word which seems to makes sense: "Hold."

Don't fall apart.

Don't lose your fucking mind.

Hold it together.

Ten minutes go by before my hand is steady enough to put the key in the ignition and drive away.

*****

Hindsight and conscience rips and tears at me. Not them, never them. Her. I'd given Audrey the worst years of my life and those same years are what I now have left to live with. I try to tell myself that if she'd left me on her own, because of the man I was, I wouldn't feel this way because at least she would still be alive. She would have moved on and eventually, I'd have done the same.

Nothing is a lie if you truly believe it.

Only I couldn't.

*****

Booze and blow, blow and booze. I'd left a running tab with Full Time Freddy and orders to keep product coming until my funds dried up and my credit was gone.

Till there is nothing left.

Drifting. Days turning into weeks of highs and lows, fear and depravation. The phone ringing, me hiding— paranoia at its zenith: It's Audrey and she knows about my transgressions. The sweet Lord has told her why our lives turned out this way and now she's angry. She wants to hear the truth from me.

Two weeks in, I rip the phone cord from the wall. It still rings. I chug bourbon. I loop one end of the cord around my neck, the other around a bedpost. Ease into it. Feel that cord go tight around my neck. Feel my head getting light. Feel that badass floating sensation.

Feel that cheap-ass cord go *snap!*

On my feet and screaming: "Now what, nigga!"

Flip the bed over. Turn the chest of drawers into kindling. Beat your head against the wall until blood's running in your eyes and down your chin.

Blood blind and raging: "Now what nigga!"

Closet, top shelf. Grab the 9mm, shove it in your eye, pull the trigger—*click—click—click*. Check the clip and stare in disbelief—what clip?

On my knees, blood dripping on the floor, nothing left. I taste the blood on my lips and mutter to someone I used to know: "Now what nigga?"

Five weeks and fifteen lost pounds later, I hear a knock at the door. Judas window view gives me little Jenny

Hughes standing on the concrete landing in a little pink dress and little black shoes over frilly white socks, hands behind her back. The world behind and around her is a radiant summer yellow and hurts my eyes.

I hesitate. I run my sticky tongue over sticky teeth. I haven't showered or shaved in weeks. The living room is a reeking pigsty. Delivery food boxes filled with moldy food litter the house. Empty bottles of booze stand like desert sentinels watching over the drifts of coke residue on the coffee table. Curtains pulled. Room dark. The a/c is turned down to seventy, countering the subtropical heat outside and I'm freezing.

Hand on the doorknob. My teeth rattle with the cocaine shakes as a voice inside my head begs: "Please don't do it!"

Betraying myself—you crazy looped-up nigger.

I open the door and Jenny walks in with a large manila envelope appearing in her hand. She turns on a living room lamp I haven't used for a year.

Pushing a pizza box aside, I sit on the couch and wrap myself in a blanket. Jenny's picked a picture off the coffee table. Two faces I don't recognize anymore are smiling against the backdrop of a blue clear sky. She puts the picture down, looks at the hole in the wall and the mess on the floor I never bothered to clean up. Then she turns to me, speaking in a voice as timid as she is small.

"I wanted to die, you know. All that time. I'm scared most all the time, even now, Mr. James. I still don't sleep so well and my stomach always hurts...but I know..." She stops and bunches her eyebrows and tightens her lips as if she's searching for a word or an answer and hoping maybe I can provide one or the other.

And then it starts, her tiny hands gripping her pink dress. She's pleading with me.

"Hmmmmmmmmmmm."

She can't stop and she's looking at me and I'm falling apart at the fucking seams. I want to ask how she knows my name, how she found me and how I can possibly respond to the horror she's been through and will continue to go through. Only I can't look at her, can't talk to her. All I can hear is her throbbing hum. My hands go to my ears and I press down tight.

Her hand falls light on my arm. I push her away until she puts both arms around me and pulls me close and I'm crying like a baby on her shoulder, telling my life's story to a twelve-year-old girl.

Audrey.

The money.

The bloody reprisal.

All of it.

Twenty minutes go by before I can pull myself together. Jenny's stopped humming, but doesn't say a word. She doesn't tell me everything will be okay.

Before leaving, Jenny hands me the envelope. I follow her to the door and see a car waiting for her. Sergeant Brice at the wheel of a navy blue unmarked. He gives me a wave. I hold up my hand and watch the two of them drive away into a bleached-out horizon.

I open the envelope. A school photo of Jenny. Her dark brown hair in pigtail braids with something passing itself off as a smile drifting across her pale face like clouds moving across the sun. She's trying to tell me everything is all right, only those baby blue eyes deceive and fail to contain her innocuous lies.

I turn my eyes up to the bright sky and then to the brilliant colors of white blossom oleander and rusty crotons growing in my own and neighboring lawns. The sun is warm on my face.

I put the picture back in its envelope, go inside and lock the door. When once again safe in the darkness of my bedroom, I slip Jenny's photograph into Audrey's book and proceed to drink and pray and hate myself into a sweet and bottomless oblivion.

*****

Two months down and the cycle repeats itself. I try to right the wrongs. For myself. For others. I hope life will work out for people like Jenny at least.

I live off my hope.

Exercise has taken the place of hate. No, nothing can fully take the place of that. I try, though. I take long runs and I lift weights and I sweat out the anger. Some of it, anyhow.

I've talked hours with my old Sarge over beers and bourbon. Brice confessed how he knew it was me who found the Hughes girl. Said it wasn't easy. The girl couldn't give a useful description, save for he was black and tall and had dark wet spots the size of silver dollars on his knees. And he stunk like hell. That was all she remembered. The detectives chalked up her fuzzy memory to post traumatic shock. The girl was safe, the bad guys were dead and the case was put in the back of a random file cabinet somewhere downtown.

Only Brice put the timing of my exit from the force and Jenny's scant description to work. He knew the whole story that morning I stood in his office. My knees. My car. My fetid smell. But he let it die a fast death on an official level.

A few weeks later he showed my picture to the girl and now the three of us hold a secret bonded in blood.

And against doubts new and old, I still pray to God, Falconer in my hands, Audrey in my hands. My knees will never stop bleeding and the terrazzo floor will always be cold and hard. But I continue waiting, knowing full well that God and Morpheus and booze will never let me have her. I know this.

I'll live out my days and nights reaching and grabbing for her in a blood red world left untouched evermore by a clean white sun. Audrey, only a few steps away, but never within reach. Her smile. Her clean sweet scent. Her iridescent green eyes and soft brown skin.

Halcyon days are gone forever.

Spinning free.

Luck
by Johnny Shaw

Violence Cortez is not a subtle man. His nickname, neck tattoo, body language, and facial expression all communicate the same thing. The same word. The same danger. Nothing clever or open to misinterpretation for this guy. Violence is violence.

Closer to a yellowjacket than a rattlesnake, Violence has a reputation for his no-quit tenacity, rage-fueled insanity that makes him avoided as much as feared. The kind of erratic personality that makes everyone nervous, that can turn a good night bad. Violence likes to brawl, an avid hobbyist, needing little more than a sideways glance to start round one. If that's your kind of fun, all the power to you. But most folks would rather have a good time.

Most folks, but not Scrote Henning, Violence's only friend. Somewhere between a sidekick and a toady, the inseparable duo spend their evenings mining every ounce of havoc from the night and a whiskey bottle.

But when the front door of the Top Hat Saloon swings open and Violence stomps in alone, the last thing the bartender Marco is thinking about is Scrote, figuring he'll show up soon enough. Marco says a soft prayer that Violence doesn't aggravate the hangover that he's been nursing all day. Sometimes all you can do is hope your trailer is standing after the tornado. You can't run, hide, or fight a force of nature. You can only have enough good luck to survive it.

Marco cracks open a Coors Light, sets it on the bar just as Violence sits, and acts like he's happy to see the dumb psychopath.

"You seen Scrote? Scrote Henning?" Violence asks.

"There more than one Scrote?"

"Don't know. Could be. You seen him?"

Marco shakes his head. "Ain't seen him since when you two were in. What was that? A week, ten days?"

Violence nods, his eyes never leaving Marco's. "You sure you're telling me the truth?"

Heat rises to Marco's face. Having his word challenged is not something he trucks with easily. But looking at Violence—eye twitching, breathing forced—Marco douses the flames with a big splash of What The Fuck Are You Doing?

"Got no reason to lie," Marco says through a strained smile.

"Everyone's got a reason to lie," Violence says with his own smile, albeit one that would make a child cry. "Just saying. You're pals with Scrote, kind of. Maybe he tells you to tell me you ain't seen him. Like that. You being a friend."

"We ain't friends, really. Just a guy I see. A guy who comes in the bar. If you don't know where he is, I sure as hell don't."

"Yeah, that's the thing. Can't find him. Ain't heard from him in days."

"Maybe something's wrong?"

"Sure as hell is. Because when I find him, I'm going to kill the son of a bitch."

*****

Issue 1

Violence Cortez and Scrote Henning leaned against Scrote's Filipino-blue Toyota pickup in the parking lot of the FastTrip, drinking tall boys and chucking the empties in the truck bed. Neither would go so far as to call it a ritual, but since Violence got back from up north, this was how they spent their Saturday nights. Other than the casinos, there wasn't much else to do in Indio. And neither man had extra money to gamble.

"Some people just got more luck than others. More good luck. More bad luck. Luck wouldn't be a word if it weren't a real thing." After ten beers, Scrote always leaned toward philosophizing and pontificating. He wasn't smart, but he had ideas. "We, the two of us, you and me, we've always had bad luck. Not our fault none of the things that happened."

"I don't buy that shit." Violence spit on the ground. "I ain't no puppet, got no choice. I control me and mine. Big difference between bad luck and a fuck-up. Give me a smoke."

Scrote dug out his pack and handed it to Violence. "Just saying, if I wouldn't've had the bad luck three years ago—Connie coming home early on the one day I was finally able to talk Sinnamon off the pole at Hot Lipps and back to my house, then I'd still be married and a regular dad and all. Like getting struck by lightning. Bad luck. Couldn't be anything else. I mean, you remember Sinnamon. Not like I had a choice."

Violence shook his head and lit the smoke, but let Scrote continue.

"And you, you're saying it wasn't bad luck the cops pulled into the parking lot of Dirty Pete's? Just as you was punishing Israel Ramirez for being an asshole—or whatever reason I'm sure he had coming?"

"He said Poison rocked harder than Metallica."

"Exactly. Capital offense. On any other night, Izzy just would've took that beating. No harm. Free ambulance ride. Stitches and plaster. But soon as a cop sees a guy

101

pummeling another guy with a stop sign, they know they can frame him on some bullshit charge. Bad luck got you four years for assault."

"And an extra year for destruction of county property." Violence laughed and gave his buddy a hard slap on the back. "You're an idiot, Scrote. A straight-up retard. But God love you, you're always ready to take a buddy's side. No matter how stupid."

Violence held up his can, Scrote tapped his against it, and they both downed the remainder of the beers. The clang of empty against empty signaled their need for more.

*****

Violence drives past the FastTrip, but there are no cars parked out front. No sparkly blue pickup, that's for sure. It's Saturday night. It's where Scrote should be. Hell, it's where Violence should be, drinking and shooting the shit. They never even had to call to meet up. It was their routine, tradition. Now Violence is sure that Scrote is avoiding him. And if Scrote isn't dead in a ditch, he's going to wish he was.

Other than drinking with Violence, Scrote only has one other thing in his life. Strippers. But Violence can't remember the name of the dancer that Scrote is banging. What is it with that idiot and strippers? It's probably the tits. They all have tits. And that's a big deal to a guy like Scrote.

Violence can't even remember her stage name. Always something spelled all squirrelly. He might even know a stripper named Squirrelly. He knows a Kanddee. A Lexxxi with three x's. And most of the spice rack: Sage, Cayenne, Saffron, Pepper, Cumin, and of course, Nutmeg. Hell, what does it matter? Not like he can look it up in the phone book. But he can head over to Hot Lipps. He knows her by sight, tramp stamp and all. Eventually, Scrote will show up. That's where the tits are.

Issue 1

Violence smiles as he turns right on the next street, thinking about tits and punishment.

*****

Scrote pulled three bags of Fritos off the chip rack. Violence knocked them out of his hands onto the floor. Neither man bothered to pick them up.

"What was that for?" Scrote asked.

"I ain't gonna smell Frito breath the rest of the night. Smells like a rendering plant. Might as well fart in my mouth and get it done with."

"I got to eat. I'm hungry."

"Jesus Christ." Violence scanned the store and pointed at a display of cookies. "Grab some Oreos or Chips Ahoy. Anything but Nutter Butters. They're worse than Fritos."

"I was more in the mood for savory," Scrote said with a bit of pout, but he walked to the cookies.

Violence set his two six-packs of tall boys on the counter in front of the bored teenager. "And a pack of Marlboros."

"You should buy a lottery ticket. I can prove my point," Scrote yelled out behind him.

"What point?" Violence said, watching his buddy dump an armload of cookies on the counter.

"About good luck and bad luck. I'll bet if you buy a lottery ticket, you won't win nothing. Because you got bad luck. Born under a bad sign, like that. If you had good luck, you'd win, right?"

"Not exactly scientific. One try? That wouldn't prove diddly-shit, dumbass. Most people don't win. You saying most people got bad luck."

"From what I can see? Yeah. The world is mostly bad luck. There'd be more people living in mansions, driving nice cars, if people had good luck. Shit, how many you know that got jobs? Ain't done time?"

Violence turned to the teenager. "The beer, the cookies, and one of them scratchers. The one with Elvis on it."

Back at the truck, Violence and Scrote each shotgunned a beer, followed by a beer chaser. Scrote pulled out a sleeve of Oreos and they had a contest to see how many they could fit in their mouth, laughing through the black crumbs.

After he chewed and swallowed, Scrote said, "Aren't you going to check your ticket?"

Violence shrugged and pulled it out of his pocket. "So if I win a free ticket, does that mean I have good luck?"

"Only if that ticket wins. Money is the scorecard for good luck. More money you got, more good luck," Scrote said, "but I'm telling you, we're both cursed, brother. You'll see."

Violence dug his fingernail into the lottery ticket and scratched. There were six numbers. He had to match two of them. The most he could win was $50,000 dollars. He scratched them in order.

The first three:

$2.

$100

$10,000

"What if I win two bucks? Barely feels like nothing. Hell, the ticket cost me a dollar. One dollar profit don't really seem like good luck."

The second three:

$50

$5

$10,000

"Well, fuck me. I think I won," Violence said, blowing some of the silver dust off the ticket.

"How much?" Scrote asked, leaning in to take a look at the ticket.

"Ten thousand bucks."

"Did you have to match two or three?"

Issue 1

"Two. It says right here," Violence said, pointing at the instructions at the top of the ticket.

"You won," Scrote said softly.

Violence read the instructions at the top of the ticket two more times. "I just won ten motherfucking grand, you silly son of a bitch. Who's got bad luck?"

*****

Violence cruises past the enormous Mexican working the door and stomps into Hot Lipps. The crowd is surprisingly sparse for a Saturday, mostly loners with eyes focused on the bored, too-skinny addict on the stage. The drunk campesino that accidentally bumps into Violence doesn't know how lucky he is. Violence is so focused that he only stomps on the guy's foot and gives him a sharp punch to the liver, letting him off easy.

As the poor bastard pukes and collapses behind him, Violence walks to the bar and orders a beer. He scans the stage and scattered audience through squinted eyes.

The deejay lowers the volume of "Dr. Feelgood" and as the boy-shaped stripper on stage collects the loose ones, he rolls out his patter. "All right, boys. Give it up for Credenza. Man, I'd like to get in her drawers. Am I right? Now we got something extra special for you, a terrible twosome, a deviant duet, a…two naked girls. Let's hear it for Domminno and Jeniniana."

When the girls reach the spotlight at the pole to shake their asses, Violence doesn't recognize either of them. Violence drinks his beer and tries to enjoy the show. The girls can dance. He likes that they still got some baby fat on them, too. Makes them look real, not all fake and artificial and plastic. He can imagine that there's plenty to hold onto.

He can feel his rod getting stiff, but that only angers him more. Just another thing that he has no control over.

The familiar pressure of fuck-or-fight is building, that's for damn sure.

He can't help but turn his head every time the front door opens, but it's never Scrote. It's either a dude who keeps his eyes to the floor or a group of drunk dudes playing grabass with each other and acting like they're seeing tit for the first time. He hates those guys. It's like they don't see how special a place like Hot Lipps is. Like they think it's some kind of joke.

When Violence got raised from Chino, the first place he went was a strip club. He wasn't ready to get laid, but he just needed to see a live, naked lady. It was scary and therapeutic and sacred. The girls didn't want nothing but money, and for that they helped bring him back into the world. It was beautiful.

Now he finds himself staring hate at three thick-necked jocks in Ed Hardy shirts and backward baseball caps. They're goofing on the dancers, making barking sounds. They're just what he needs. Picking on some little guy wouldn't be satisfying. But three gym punks, this should be interesting.

Before he even knows it himself, he's standing over the three jocks' table. "You boys consider yourself lucky?"

The three boys look up at him, scoping his prison ink. One of them glances to the bouncer, who is distractedly texting.

The biggest of the three speaks up. "What? What do you want?"

"Do you think you got good luck or bad luck?"

"The fuck? We're here to watch the strippers. Not to talk to some faggot about whatever the fuck. Go away, asshole."

"Fair enough. Answered the question for me."

"What the fuck are you talking about?"

"You got bad luck, son. That's what you got," Violence says smiling. "Not even my fault. Just your luck."

"Fu—"

Issue 1

Violence grabs the back of the kid's head and slams his face against the table, blood flying in an arc as he lifts it back up. He slams his head down again. The boy to his right tries to push away from the table and stand, but Violence kicks out, connecting with the kid's knee. The strippers on stage turn when they hear the liquidy pop. The short one pukes when she sees the damage.

The kid to the left gets one good shot at Violence, but he blows it. He throws a huge haymaker that only grazes Violence's jaw. The expression on his face says it all, knowing what's coming next. Pain and punishment.

Violence keeps the mystery short, grabbing the guy by the crotch and lifting him off the ground as he squeezes. The kid's scream-grunt sounds like a hernia feels.

Out of the corner of his eye, Violence sees the bouncer making his way to the table, pushing patrons and chairs out of the way. He looks like an elephant charging through high grass.

"Maybe you got a little good luck, kid. Remember that. If all you had was bad luck, I'd be taking your balls with me."

Lifting by the crotch with one hand and grabbing the front of his shirt with the other, he turns the kid's body and throws the big kid at the bouncer. And while the toss doesn't quite reach the bouncer, landing on the ground at his feet, the shock of having a person thrown at him is enough to allow Violence to escape through the fire exit.

*****

"Shit." Violence threw his beer can against the side of the truck. "I can't win this. Can't win no lottery."

"Why? What's wrong?" Scrote asked, watching the wasted beer drain onto the ground.

"Maybe you were right about bad luck," Violence said, "I can't win the lottery."

"What're you talking about? You just did."

"It's gambling. It's a violation of my parole. Any kind of gambling. If I try to get my money, not only won't they give it to me, they'll throw me back inside."

"The lottery ain't gambling. It's legal and shit. The government runs it, and the government can't do anything illegal. They make the laws."

"They make the rules, too." Violence lit a fresh cigarette off his old one, laughed to himself, then grabbed the front of Scrote's shirt. "But nothing says you can't gamble."

"Sure. I gamble all the time. Blackjack, Pai Gow. Don't understand craps though."

"You can mail the ticket in, get the money. I'll give you a commission. Say…ten percent. One grand. Just to use your name and get the cash."

"A grand? Sure."

Violence pulled the ticket out of his pocket, looking at the matching numbers for the fiftieth time. He handed it to Scrote. "Don't lose it. And don't even think about trying to run off with that money."

Scrote looked hurt. "I wouldn't never do that."

"Because I would fucking kill you. Money makes people stupid sometimes."

"We're friends. Money ain't worth more than that. It won't make me stupid."

"Naw, you already are."

Violence laughed and Scrote followed his lead. Violence cracked a fresh beer and held it to the air. "To good luck."

*****

Still amped after the fight in the strip club, Violence cruises Indio, eyes out for Scrote or his truck. After an hour and out of ideas, he heads home. He's still angry, but it's the kind of angry that soothes like a blanket on a cold day. It sharpens his mind, focuses his revenge, and strengthens his resolve. He knows he isn't going to stop until he finds Scrote and punishes him.

Turning down his street, his headlights flash off the glitter-blue of Scrote's truck at the end of the block. Parked right in front of his house.

"Well, I'll be goddamned."

Violence floors it, jumps the curb, and slides his truck across his own lawn. It's just dirt and scattered weeds, so there's no grass to destroy. Scrote stands up from the front step, eyes wide.

Violence jumps out of his truck, twenty-inch, six-D-Cell Maglite in hand.

Scrote holds up his hands. "Wait. I know you're pissed. I can explain."

But before Scrote can get out another word, Violence swings the flashlight, hitting him in the neck. Scrote falls, gasping for breath and clutching at his neck. The fresh wound immediately turns a deep red-purple.

Violence doesn't let up. He moves to Scrote's pelvis and legs, pounding the flashlight down onto his limbs. Skin and muscle only act as minimal padding, the contact sounding like metal on bone. Scrote's attempts at screams come out as wheezing gasps, painful and sickly.

After one particularly hard blow, the head of the flashlight breaks off and the batteries fly from the long tube.

Violence steps back, breathing hard from the exertion. He puts one hand on a knee, shaky. When Scrote reaches out to him, he knocks the hand away and stomps on it with his boot, snapping the fingers.

Violence yells through spit and anger. His eyes tear up. "How long we been friends? How long? And you shit on our good times for money? For ten fucking grand? One thousand of which was yours. So you fucked me for nine grand, really. That's your price, you cheap son of a bitch?"

Scrote tries to talk, but only bloody bubbles froth from his mouth.

Violence continues, "Money is money. I get that. But shit, if you would've said, 'I need the money for an operation' or some shit, I would've given it to you. I would've given you all of it and whatever else I had. It's money. That's all. Friends is more important than money, dumbass. You said that shit yourself."

"Didn't steal nothin', Violence," Scrote finally gets out.

"Then hand over my dough."

Scrote shakes his head.

"Right. What happened? You lose it at the casino? Same difference. You been ducking me. You ain't got the money. That's stealing in anyone's book."

"Bad luck. It was just bad luck," Scrote says.

"Fuck you."

"They took it."

"Don't tell me it got stole. Don't bullshit me. You do that and you're going to get really hurt."

Scrote tries to reach into his pocket, but his broken fingers only flop against his shirt pocket. He gives up, looking at Violence. "In there."

Violence leans down and reaches in Scrote's pocket, pulling out an envelope. It's from the State Lottery Board. He pulls out the letter inside. He mumble-reads through the letter, "Dear Mr. Henning. Due to overdue child support. Lottery winnings will be issued to…Oh, *hell* no."

Scrote nods his head, and then rests it on the concrete. "My neck feels really weird. Like it hurts, but it doesn't."

"Those fucks. Why didn't you say something? What kind of asshole don't pay child support?"

"Never had the money. Didn't know they'd know. Didn't think of it."

"If the state took the cash, why'd you duck me? Why didn't you call and tell me? Why'd you avoid me? You must've known I'd think you took it."

"When you get mad, you get scary. I thought if I let some time pass, you'd calm down."

"I calmed down all right."

"I was embarrassed. That's why I came over. To tell you. To your face. Show you the letter. Say I'm sorry."

Violence shakes his head. He looks down at his friend. The swelling of Scrote's leg is visible even under his jeans. And his neck is every color it shouldn't be. More than a bruise, maybe a broken blood vessel or something. It looks like he just swallowed a water balloon that got caught on the way down.

Violence gets his arms underneath Scrote and lifts him up. Scrote groans, red drool trailing to the ground.

"Maybe that nurse you like will be working the emergency room tonight," Violence says.

"Sheila."

"She the one with the big tits?"

"You know me."

Violence sets Scrote in the passenger seat of his truck and buckles him in. He jumps into the driver's side and starts the engine.

"It's all my fault," Scrote says, "should've never tried our luck knowing it was bad."

"Shut up and bleed quieter," Violence says. "You owe me ten grand. You know that, right?"

"Nine grand. A thousand was mine, remember?"

"Don't be an idiot. You can't get a commission on money I never got."

Violence backs his truck onto the road. Scrote yells when the truck bounces off the curb. They head east toward the hospital.

"You want I should stop by FastTrip and grab a six and some Fritos on the way to the hospital?"

"May as well. The emergency room gets busy on Saturday night."

Special Bonus!!!

The opening chapters of **THE HARD BOUNCE** by Todd Robinson, coming your way from Tyrus Books in January 2013.

Issue 1

Twenty-Three Years Ago

The Boy was eight years old when he learned how to hate.

It's still difficult, even today, for him to remember the events in their right order. He knows where they should go, but hard as he tries, they drift through his mind like glitterflakes in a sno-globe.

The screaming and the blood followed the first explosion. That much he's sure of. So much blood.

The second explosion. Running at him. Throwing himself at a grown man like a rabid animal, unaware that it doesn't stand a chance. He was big for his age. He still didn't stand a chance.

Bang. He was gone. Just like that. Tumbling in and out of consciousness with no idea where he was. What time it was. Who or where he is.

Bang. He was back. A priest. He can't understand him. The inside of an ambulance, feeling it hurtle through the Boston traffic, the doctor unable to control his tears as he tries to stem the tide of blood that won't stop pouring out of him. The Boy didn't know there was that much blood inside of him. He knew he would run out soon. He was terrified.

Bang. On a gurney. Lots of people yelling. He bites somebody's hand. A sharp pinprick in his arm. *Where is she?*

Bang. Another priest. He's saying the same unintelligible words as the first.

Months in a hospital. Pain like an eight-year-old should never know exists in this world. Parades of doctors—first for his ruined body, the second for his damaged mind.

He has an anger management problem, they say.

Anger management. It's a nice term for people who can afford it.

Psychologists in two hundred-dollar sweaters and condescending smiles, telling him:

You need to let it go.

Think about the rest of your life.

Think about how lucky you are.

The world is a beautiful place.

The world is not a beautiful place. Not to The Boy, who's going to need two more operations before he can piss without a tube and spigot.

They ask him why he's such an angry person, what he's so angry at.

Think about how lucky you are.

Chapter One

I can't tolerate a bully, even when my job is to be the biggest swinging dick on the block.

Somebody in the booking office for The Cellar thought that all-ages punk shows on the weekends was a bright idea. Maybe it was. Nobody owned up to having the idea though.

The place was crowded, high school kids with rainbow-tinted hairdos making up most of the audience. The rest were uncomfortable parents watching their babies perform in bands with names like Mazeltov Cocktail and No Fat Chicks. As far as crowds go, they were a nice break from the normal regiment of scumbags, skinheads, punks, frat boys, musicians, and wannabes that we had to deal with. Odds were pretty good we wouldn't be involved in any brawls or dragging overdoses out of the bathroom. All things considered, it should have been a cakewalk day.

Shoulda, woulda, coulda.

Me and Junior handled the shift ourselves: me watching the door while Junior patrolled the three floors of the club. Between the two of us, we could easily police a few dozen skinny tweens. We were less bouncers than babysitters with a combined weight of 470 pounds (mostly mine) and about ten grand in tattoos (mostly Junior's). Every parent's dream.

We'd only been open an hour and we'd already confiscated seventeen bottles of beer, two bottles of vodka, one of rum, three joints, and seven airplane bottles of tequila. The way it was going, Junior and I would be able to stock our own bars by nightfall.

A collective groan floated out from inside the bar as the ninth inning closed at Fenway. I poked my head in to check the score. 9-3 Yankees.

And it just had to be the fucking Yankees, didn't it?

As I poked my head back out, the first fat droplets of rain spattered on my shoes, as if the angels themselves wept for the poor Sox. I backed under The Cellar's fluorescent sign, but the wind zigzagged the drizzle all over me.

At least I was in a better place than Junior. The basement didn't have any ventilation and crowds produced furnace-level temperatures. A hot wind would gust up the stairs when the club got crowded, feeling (and smelling) like Satan farting on your back. If I was hot outside, Junior must have been miserable.

The first wave of baseball fans wandered into Kenmore Square. I could hear chants of "Yankees suck" approaching from the Fenway area.

Two guys broke off from the herd, stumbling in the bar's direction. The bigger guy wore an old Yaztremski jersey and a mullet that would have embarrassed Billy Ray Cyrus in 1994. His buddy wore a backwards old-school Patriots hat and a Muffdiving Instructor t-shirt.

Really...? Really?

Asshats.

I recognized their tribe immediately, the type of townies who will go to their graves believing they could do a better job than the pros did—if only they hadn't knocked up Mary Lou Dropdrawers senior year.

Those guys.

Mullet looked over, his eyes wide as he saw the crew of punk kids in front of The Cellar. His smile was filled with a bully's joy. He grabbed Buddy's collar and pointed his attention towards the kids.

"Nice hairdo," the townie called out to the kids milling outside. "What are you, some kinda faggot?"

I closed my eyes and sighed.

Away we go…

Buddy laughed with a mocking hilarity, pointing a finger and looking to the rest of the crowd for an approval he wasn't getting.

A skinny kid, head shaved close and dyed in a leopard skin pattern, turned. "Why? You looking for some ass, sailor?" the kid yelled back, smacking his bony behind for emphasis. He got some approving chuckles from the passersby and hoots of laughter from the other kids.

Buddy looked pissed off that the kid got the laughs from the crowd that he hadn't.

"What did you say to me, bitch?" said Mullet, quickstepping towards the bar.

The kid flipped the guy off with both hands and ran back into the club.

When Mullet got a couple of feet from the entrance, I stepped halfway across the doorway. He stopped short and we stood there, shoulder to shoulder.

"What's your problem?" Mullet asked, puffing out his chest.

"No problem," I said, blowing cigarette smoke out my nose, moving my face closer to his. "It's just not happening for you here. Not today."

"I wanna get a beer." His breath reeked of soft pretzels and a few too many overpriced Fenway Miller Lites.

"Not here you're not. Get one down the street if you're thirsty."

Buddy suddenly found his shoes real fascinating. Mullet and I kept giving each other the hairy eyeball. "It's a free country, asshole."

"And a wonderful free country it is. This bar isn't, though. Not for you. Not today." I took another long pull from my cigarette and fought the urge to blow the smoke into his face.

"Who's gonna stop me, you?"

"Yup." There it was. The frog was dropped. Let's see if it jumped. I balled my fist around the medium-point Sharpie in my pocket. Bouncer's best friend. Won't kill anybody, but hurts like a bitch when jammed between a couple of ribs.

I stood at the long end of his best intimidating stare, which frankly, wasn't. Mullet decided to give it one last shot.

"What are you? Some kind of tough guy?"

"Well, gee golly Hoss, I haven't started any fights with twelve-year-olds lately, so I'm not sure." I moved my face right into his. One more inch and my cigarette was going up his nose. I removed my hand from my pocket and held it low at my side.

Buddy grabbed Mullet's arm, and Mullet twitched like he'd been shocked.

"C'mon, man. Let's go." Buddy's voice cracked like he'd just been kicked in the nuts. Now I know why he'd minded his own. Hard to talk tough a tough line when you sound like Minnie Mouse.

"Yeah. Fine. This bar's full of faggots anyway," Mullet muttered as he walked off.

"Fuck you very much, gentlemen. Have a good one." I clipped a sharp one-fingered salute at them as they retreated.

The kids applauded and cheered as the two walked off. I shut them up quick with a glower. I made a hundred bucks a shift, plus a tip-out from the bar. Not enough money to be anybody's pal.

More noise pollution began thumping from the basement. The group quickly ground out their smokes on the wet cement as they filtered back inside.

A girl with brightly dyed red hair lingered outside longer than the rest. I could feel her stare on the side of my neck like a sun lamp. I glanced over and she gave me a little smile. She couldn't have been more than fifteen, but behind the smile was something older. Something that made me uncomfortable.

As she passed me going into the club, she brushed her tiny body against me, tiptoed up, and kissed me on the cheek. "My hero," she whispered softly into my ear and went inside.

I shuddered with Nabokovian creeps, and shifted my attention back to the crowd. (And yes, fuck you, I know who Nabokov is. I'm a bouncer, not a retard.)

I kept my thousand-yard stare front and center on the passing crowd, keeping my peripheral sharp for any run-up sucker punches. It happens. I was alert to every degree of my environment except what was directly behind me; which is why I nearly had a heart attack when a booming crash sounded from the back of the bar. Instinctively, I ducked, made sure my head was still intact. Inside the bar, every patron jerked his head toward the hallway leading to the parking lot out back. I bull-rushed through the thick crowd, almost knocking down a couple customers. Somebody's beer spilled down the seat of my pants as I hit the hallway.

Junior was halfway up the back stairs when I hit the huge steel exit door at full clip. The door opened only a couple inches before slamming into something solid, my shoulder making a wet popping sound. The door clanged like a giant cymbal and I ricocheted back, landing on top of Junior. We both toppled hard onto the concrete stairwell. Pretty pink birdies chirped in my head as I lay sprawled on top of him.

"Christ! Get offa me!" Junior yelped.

I rolled onto my wounded arm, and whatever popped in my shoulder snapped back into the socket. I roared like a gut-shot bull.

Junior pulled himself up and pressed against the door with all his weight. The door barely budged. Whatever was jammed against the door squealed metallically against the concrete.

I pinwheeled my arm a couple times to make sure there was no permanent damage. Apart from a dull throb and some numbness in my fingers, I'd survive.

"You okay?" Junior asked.

"Seems like it."

"Then do you wanna help me move this fucking thing or should I kiss your boo-boo first?"

"Would you?"

I pressed my good shoulder against the door beside Junior and pushed. Whatever was on the other side, it was heavy as hell. With a painful scraping of metal, the door slowly slid open. We had about an eighth of a second to wish it hadn't.

A flood of garbage and scumwater came pouring through the crack. Plastic cups, beer cans, crusty napkins, and a few good gallons of dumpster juice slopped over our shoes. Somebody had toppled the entire Dumpster across the entryway. The stink was epic.

"Motherfucker!" Junior dry-heaved mightily, but didn't puke. "I just bought these goddamn shoes!"

A horn honked in the parking lot. Mullet and Buddy sat in the cab of a black Ford Tundra. They were laughing their asses off and wagging middle fingers as they peeled out and shot the pickup toward the lot gate.

The truck got halfway across the lot before jamming up in the long line of exiting Sox Faithful. Other cars moved in from both sides and the rear, neatly boxing them in. They had nowhere to go.

Junior stomped across the parking lot, his temper giving him an Irish sunburn. "I'm going to kill you, then fuck you, you cocksucker!"

I'm not sure that was what Junior meant to convey, but I went with the sentiment. "That's right," I called out. "He's not gay; he just likes to fuck dead things."

In the large rearview mirrors, I could see the fear on Mullet's face. Suddenly, I saw him lean over and grab for something. I was pretty sure it wasn't going to be a kitten.

"He's reaching!" I yelled to Junior. We took the last twenty feet at a sprint, and I swung a haymaker into the open driver's side window. My fist cracked Mullet right in the back of his hairdo as he turned back.

"Gahh!" he replied. His hands were empty.

"Hey!" was all Buddy had time for before Junior reached into the passenger side, grabbed his head, and whacked his face hard onto the dashboard.

A pair of high voices cried out from the cab as two small faces in Red Sox caps smushed against the tinted glass. "Daddy!" one of the little boys cried in terror.

Bang.

The world exploded red and I had Mullet's windpipe in the middle of my squeezing fingers.

"*Are you fucking nuts?* Were you going to drive drunk with your fucking kids in the back?" Spittle flew from my lips onto Mullet's reddening face. "Are you out of your *fucking mind?*"

"Please don't hurt my daddy!" Tiny fingers clasped at mine, trying to pry them open. Something deep inside was telling me to let go, but the rest of me wasn't hearing it.

"Let him go, Boo." Junior's voice sounded miles away. I saw his hands on my arms, pulling me, but I couldn't feel him there.

Mullet's lips went blue, and his eyes started to roll up white.

Buddy was also trying frantically to loosen my grip. "Jesus Christ, you're killing him! Let him go." Buddy's blood-slicked fingers kept slipping off mine.

Suddenly, an explosion shocked my hands off Mullet's throat. I stepped back, my hands reflexively going to the place I thought I'd been shot. The truck listed down and to the left. Another explosion and the truck sank further. I wheeled my head to see Junior standing by the limp oversized tire, box-cutter in his hand. "Let's go, Boo. They're not going anywhere."

I blinked a few times, regaining myself. One of the boys was halfway though the partition into the front seat. He was crying, snot running over his upper lip, screaming at me, the monster who was hurting his daddy. "Go *away*!" he shrieked. "Go *away*!" He threw an empty Red Sox souvenir cup at me. It bounced off my chest, clattered to the ground.

Junior took me by the arm and pulled me the long way around to the entrance of The Cellar so no one could tell the cops where to find us.

Junior walked at my side as we passed around the lot. I could feel his eyes on me. Without looking over, I said, "You got something to say?"

"Nothing specific. You okay?"

"Finer than Carolina. We just performed a public service, if you ask me."

He didn't ask me. "Fair enough," he said. "You want a soda big guy?"

"Fuck off."

Toward the front of the jam, an old lady in a beat up Dodge Omni and Red Sox cap gave me a big thumbs-up.

For some reason, that bothered me.

I could still hear the kids crying when we got back to the bar. I shouldn't have been able to, but I did.

TO BE CONTINUED IN **THUGLIT #2**

AUTHOR BIOS

JORDAN HARPER was born and educated in Missouri. He has worked as a music critic and journalist, and is currently a writer for *The Mentalist* on CBS. His nonfiction has appeared in *The Village Voice* and other papers. His fiction has appeared in *Out of the Gutter* and *Crime Factory*, but *Thuglit* is his home.

JASON DUKE was a Sergeant in the U.S. Army for six years. He was deployed 15 months to Iraq from 07-09. Now he lives and writes full-time in Phoenix, Arizona. His fiction has appeared in *Plots With Guns, Thuglit, Spinetingler Magazine, Crimewav.com, Crimefactory, Needle Magazine, Yellow Mama, Darkest Before the Dawn*, and *A Twist of Noir*, among others. He also has stories in the e-anthologies *D*CKED* and *Pulp Ink* which are available on amazon.com.

COURT MERRIGAN's short story collection, *Moondog Over The Mekong*, is out soon from Snubnose Press. He's a Spinetingler Award nominee with stuff appearing or forthcoming all over. Links at http://courtmerrigan.wordpress.com. He also runs the Bareknuckles Pulp department at *Out of the Gutter* and lives in Wyoming with his family.

Issue 1

HILARY DAVIDSON is the author of *The Damage Done*, which won the Anthony Award for Best First Novel as well as a Crimespree Award. Her second novel, *The Next One to Fall*, is a thriller set in Peru.

TERRENCE P. McCAULEY won the TruTV Search for the Next Great Crime Writer contest in 2008. His manuscript, *The Slow Burn* will be published by Noir Nation Books in Summer 2012. His manuscript, *Prohibition*, will be published in Fall 2012 by Airship 27. A native of the Bronx, N.Y., he is currently working on his next novel. His blog can be found at http://terrencemccauley.blogspot.com/ and his email is terrencepmccauley@gmail.com.

MATTHEW C. FUNK is a social media consultant, editor of *Needle Magazine*, and staff writer for *Planet Fury* and *Criminal Complex*. Funk has work featured at numerous sites indexed on his Web domain and printed in *Needle*, *Grift*, *Pulp Modern*, *Pulp Ink* and *D*CKED*.

MIKE WILKERSON was raised in rural Northwest Kansas and has resided in St. Petersburg, Florida for the past eleven years. His work has appeared in *The Flash Fiction Offensive* as a featured writer, (the original) *Thuglit*, *A Twist of Noir* and *Thrillers, Killers and Chillers*. He is currently working on a crime novel and more of his work can be found on his blog: Writing The Hard Way.

JOHNNY SHAW was born and raised on the Calexico/Mexicali border, the setting for his novels, *Dove Season: A Jimmy Veeder Fiasco*, and the upcoming *Big Maria*. He is also the editor and a regular contributor for the fiction quarterly, Blood & Tacos. You can follow Johnny's exploits at jhonnyshaw.com or on Twitter at @BloodAndTacos.

TODD ROBINSON (Editor) is the creator and Chief Editor of *Thuglit*. His writing has appeared in *Blood & Tacos*, *Plots With Guns*, *Needle Magazine*, *Shotgun Honey*, *Strange, Weird, and Wonderful*, *Out of the Gutter*, *Pulp Pusher*, *Grift*, *Demolition Magazine*, *CrimeFactory* and the anthologies *Lost Children: Protectors*, and *Danger City*. He has been nominated for a Derringer Award, short-listed for *Best American Mystery Stories*, selected for Writers Digest's Year's Best Writing 2003 and won the inaugural Bullet Award in June 2011. The first collection of his short stories, *Dirty Words* is now available as an E-book and his debut novel *The Hard Bounce* will be released in January 2013 from Tyrus Books.

ALLISON GLASGOW (Editor) Hates you.

Issue 1

Made in the USA
Columbia, SC
11 September 2021

45310221R00081